Confessions of a MadMan

From Madison Avenue To Island Sands

Confessions of a MadMan From Madison Avenue to Island Sands © 2009 Miller Pope

All rights reserved. No material in this book may be copied or reproduced in any manner without the express written consent of the author.

Published by Island Press
310 E. First Street
Ocean Isle Beach NC 28469
www.millerpope.com

Cover and interior design: Miller Pope
Cover illustration: Miller Pope
Interior illustrations: Miller Pope

Printed in USA

LIBRARY OF CONGRESS CATALOGING-IN-PUBLICATION DATA

Pope, Miller.

Confessions of a MadMan From Madison Avenue to Island Sands © 2009 Miller Pope
Miller Pope; illustrated by the author.

ISBN 978-1-61539-774-7

Preface

Every life has a story — this is mine. Much of it dwells with the main stream of life in the fast paced world of art and advertising during the years following the Second World War. This book has some of my old illustrations and photographs, as well as a few drawings made specifically for this book.

Many thanks are owed to Volkswagen, Coca-Cola, and The American Tobacco Company for the use of their ads. I am also indebted to Jack DeGroot, Ken Buckner, Peggy and Jim Grich, and many others for their encouragement and help with this book.

Very little research was required as these events are burned into my memory. Except for the use of the internet to check a few dates, the things spoken here are as fresh in my mind as if they had happened yesterday. A few names have been changed for my protection, although it is unlikely that many of these people are still living.

To my grandchildren
Sydney
Jessica
John
Chasen

Contents

Chapter One ...	Debut	page	1
Chapter Two ...	War	page	20
Chapter Three ...	The Corps	page	30
Chapter Four ...	The Black Hole	page	53
Chapter Five ...	A Tied Knot	page	57
Chapter Six ...	Think Small	page	84
Chapter Seven ...	Teeming Talent	page	101
Chapter Eight ...	Puddle Jump	page	110
Chapter Nine ...	Dream House	page	122
Chapter Ten ...	España	page	150
Chapter Eleven ...	Milestones	page	167
Chapter Twelve ...	The Island	page	180
Chapter Twelve ...	Fortune's Smile	page	198

Debut

In early April 1959 a black and white ad appeared for a strange looking little German automobile. Many if not most people considered the car to be very ugly. The little vehicle had been designed at the behest of Adolph Hitler in 1936 to populate his new Autobahn system and the ad was created by an all-Jewish ad agency which existed amid the Ivy League W.A.S.P. dominated advertising world of the time. The ad turned the advertising world on its head. It was also a major factor in making the Volkswagen beetle the best selling motor car of all time.

The three decades following the second world war were a golden age for the men know as hucksters, ad men or mad men (a contraction of Madison Avenue and advertising).

The American people were younger than at any time in our history, better educated and growing more mobile. The future looked very bright as we elected our youngest president and we began the exploration of space.

I had one foot in this exciting new advertising era and the other in the equally new era of publishing. This is my story lived amid the advertising world of Madison Avenue and the publishing world of New York and Boston during this period of great creativity and change.

The Twentieth century was still young when I made my debut on the world stage. 1929, my first year witnessed the curtain drop on the "Roaring Twenties." It dropped with a mighty crash on Wall Street.

I was born that fateful year in Greenville, South Carolina on the eighth day of April. The great "War to end all wars" had ended only eleven years before and Confederate veterans still marched in parades.

My life has not been one great big party! But that's the way I remember it. Perhaps adventure is a better word than party. There were some hard times and some miserable times. There were even some hungry times but they are not what I remember. I remember the good times. I remember all the good people who will always live on as long as I have breath.

The Zen Buddhists have a saying "The journey is the reward." To me this is a profound utterance. It has been my luck to have begun my journey in the best country ever devised by man. And in the generation which spans most of the last century of the second millennium. My sojourn even spans a small portion of the third millennium. A trip which debuted with horses will exit with rockets to the stars.

It is true that I missed the first quarter of the nineteenth century however, its essence was still around when I stepped on stage. Horse drawn wagons delivered ice and fresh bread in towns throughout the land. Plows drawn by horses and mules were more common than tractors. The US Calvary didn't ride in tanks and fly in helicopters. They rode horses!

Outhouses were common even in some cities. Most of today's household appliances weren't even dreamed of and most rural homes were lighted at night by kerosene lamps.

There were great compensations for the lack of television and airlines. Most people never locked their doors. Food tasted better because it wasn't full of things like monosodium glutamate.

Travel by auto took a lot longer than now, but it was more interesting. Every mile didn't look like every other mile as it does on an interstate today. You never knew what was around the next corner. Air conditioning in a car was unimagined and few autos even had heaters. We rode with the windows open in the summer and we had lap robes for the

Wondrous sights sped by the windows

winter. Somehow it was more fun.

Travel by train was the way to go and here was truly high adventure! From the arrival at the depot with the crowds of people, the busy baggage handlers in their bright red caps, the mighty locomotive panting steam in its static grandeur, to the booming voice of the loud speaker announcing exotic destinations . . . everything moved toward the great crescendo . . . the departure!

The departure was heady stuff. First came the exciting cry of the conductor . . . All Aboard, All Aboard! Sweethearts kissed, friends and relatives embraced before jumping aboard. The huge iron clad beast released a cloud of steam. Slowly the wheels of the great leviathan would spin a little as they sought traction. The entire train of cars would ease forward. Then with a mighty chug the huge gears of the locomotive would begin to move faster and faster. Soon you were settled back listening to the clickety clack of the unwelded rails and the steady chug of steam power. Every once in a while the wonderful sound of the great steam whistle would punctuate the air. What joy!

The luxurious way to go overnight by train was in a Pullman car.

Unfortunately, I never experienced travel in this manner. First of all we never went far enough. Secondly it probably would have been too expensive. I have always regretted that this experience was denied me. However, travel in the day coach was not to be sneered at. Wondrous sights sped by the windows. Tunnels plunged the train into mysterious darkness. High trestles supplied delicious sheer terror. Occasionally the long snake of cars made a sufficiently sharp turn to reveal the mighty engine chugging in the distance. It was worth the risk of a cinder in the eye to lean out the window for a better view. And every now and then came the shrill thunder of that splendid whistle.

People enshrined in Pullman cars dined on Duck L'Orange, but we had better fare. We had my mother's fried chicken, buttermilk biscuits and freshly baked chocolate cake. Pity the poor Pullman car riders!

Those passengers who did not possess a treasure trove of culinary goodies did not die of starvation. Men plied the isles of the train laden with sandwiches, candy and other eats as well as magazines and newspapers. Perhaps the passing of the age of steam marks the passing of the age of romance.

As I look back on the America of my youth many things seem to contradict themselves. The country was still in the throws of the great depression with millions out of work. At the same time there was no doubt in anyone's mind that this was the best, freest, most powerful country on earth. Most people had to scrimp and save and work long hours to survive, but the heroes and heroines of the most popular moving pictures were rich and carefree. And they flitted about spending money with gay abandon. The westerns, the exotic adventure movies and a handful of films made from classic novels or plays such as *The Grapes of Wrath* were the exception. The movie viewers wanted escape. They didn't want to bask in misery.

You could always count on two things when you went to see a picture show. Everything came up roses at the end and the heavies got their comeuppance.

The southerners of my youth were just as fiercely patriotic and as proud as other Americans of the United States. But at the same time we were very different. We were also patriotic citizens of yet another country. We owed an allegiance to an invisible country — Dixieland — The South!

We had our own speech, we had our own food and we had our own customs. More than anything else we had our own memories and pride. Confederate veterans still marched in parades. Every family still had its stories about the horrid Yankees and the exploits of dashing confederate ancestors.

My aunt, Mary Charles Maxwell, a prominent patrician of New Bern, North Carolina possessed a devilish streak and enjoyed shocking fellow members of The Daughters of the Confederacy. After hearing them go on at great length about their great ancestor Colonel So-and-So, their great ancestor General So-and-So or their great ancestor Major So-and-So, she would proclaim her decent from the only private in the Confederate Army! Then she would comment upon the remarkable fact that our noble army had held off all those damn Yankees for four years with only one brave private soldier!

My parents kept a goat in the back yard. The goat was probably a lifesaver for me. I had been weaned from Mother's milk and I was allergic to cow's milk.

That's about all I know about our home in Greenville. It was no doubt small because my father earned very little. He was the black sheep of a prominent Greenville family and he had run away from home rather than go to medical school as desired by my grandmother.

Grandmother Pope had a very quiet and dour personality but was a good and kind person. As a proud southern lady of the old school she strived to retain the manners and dignity of her aristocratic upbringing. Her father had become a very wealthy mercantile merchant after his service in the Confederate Army. Upon his death she had inherited a portion of his wealth.

Grandfather Pope's father was a Baptist Minister who had served as a chaplain in the Confederate army. Just short of his graduation, his senior year at the Princeton Theological Seminary was cut short by the outbreak of war.

As a preacher's son, my grandfather was considered the social equal of my grandmother. Preachers were socially accepted but not very financially very well off. My grandfather, who wanted to become a lawyer, had his dream abruptly halted when his father died. Young Tom Pope had to forgo college and go to work to support his mother and family.

He found a six day week, ten hour-a-day job as a salesman in a haberdashery. He was so eager to sell that he would stand out on the wooden sidewalk and practically pull people into the store!

He fell madly in love with young Kate Miller and she with him. When he made a delivery to her house in his capacity as a delivery boy he had to use the service entrance but when he visited her socially he used the main entrance. They were married and had a long and happy marriage. This was despite my grandfather eventually losing my grandmother's money in a series of businesses.

Thomas and Katherine Pope had six children all of whom went to college except for my father. They were all engaged in intellectual pursuits except, for my father. He was the consummate he- man who hated school and all things intellectual. He was a rugged outdoor man who seemed immune to pain or discomfort. If only he had been born a century or two earlier he would have made a wonderful Daniel Boone or Davie Crocket. He was a kind and loving father but he and I were cut out of different cloth. I was a throw back to my grandfather Pope who loved literature, history,

My father

Mother with her brother and sister

Grandfather Pope

Grandfather Hunt

politics and learning. Perhaps the largest difference I had with my father was my love of comfort.

Dad had left home and taken a job working in a bakery. He met and married my mother Lucille Hunt. She was the daughter of Walter Hunt, a conductor on the Southern Railroad. She was thus not of the same social strata as my father's family. This of course mattered not a bit to my father and they began a love affair that lasted a lifetime.

Mother was full to the brim with joie de vie and a real hoot. She could create much out of nothing and was the life of every party. She spouted witticisms like a machine gun spouts bullets. She had no regard for accuracy. To get at the truth you had to divide everything she said by at least ten.

My mother's mother, Maude Hunt, died when I was very young. I don't remember much about her. She was tied to a wheelchair but she seemed to be always cheerful and could keep me laughing.

Grandfather Hunt was a true character. He was always immaculately dressed even in his railroad overalls. They were always perfectly clean and well pressed with the creases perfectly aligned. His multitude of shoes were always well shined. He was tall and well proportioned. In his suit and tie, which he always wore when not at work, he looked the part of a true gentleman of the old South.

He was a country connoisseur. He cured his own hams, which had to come from pigs that weighed 200 pounds and preferably had been fed acorns. His honey could only come from Indians he knew in the mountains and his liquor had to come from a moonshiner he knew. He would personally inspect the still and approve the product. He didn't like legal whiskey because he said it was "chemical whiskey" and could kill you.

Grandfather Hunt ate only small portions but he had to have the table groaning with a wide selection of food. There would always be a variety of desserts but he never ate them. He always finished his meal with black strap molasses and butter on a hot biscuit. Before their application to the biscuit the butter and molasses were carefully mixed in a ceremony that mimiced the Japanese Tea Ceremony.

After he died, his son, my uncle, showed me a faded article from *The New York Times* dated around the turn of the century. It concerned my grandfather. It stated that he was the subject of a medical miracle. He had survived a stab in the brain with an ice pick without any brain damage. Some one had stabbed him in the back of the head one dark night at the train depot. I can only imagine that the ice pick must have gone exactly between the two lobes of his brain or I probably would not be here.

Some of the hobos who rode freight trains were dangerous back then, trains were sometimes robbed. For that reason he carried a German Lugger, from WWII, in a shoulder holster when he was at work.

Both my grandfathers always carried canes even though they did not need them for walking. It was just what gentlemen did in their day. They came in handy for rapping on a counter for attention in a business establishment. It was also the custom for people to carry personal cards which were left in a little silver tray when making social calls.

My grandfathers were good friends and played pinochle together even though their families didn't socialize. It has been my observation that in the south it was common for bank officers to breakfast with plumbers but their families would not dine together.

My grandfather Pope was extremely well read and always wore three piece suits, which were usually pierced by tiny holes from burning ash. The ash rained at times from his loosely packed hand rolled cigarettes. He rolled his own cigarettes in a special paper imported from France and filled them only with Prince Albert pipe tobacco. The German occupation of France in the second world war presented him with a crisis when the import of his special paper ceased. I don't remember how he dealt with this but the rain of burning ash continued to consume his suits until his demise.

He had made some good investments with my grandmother's money. The problem was that he got out at the wrong time or was caught by the depression. He and a partner had the Coca-Cola franchise for a large part of the Carolinas in the early years of Coke but then his partner divorced his wife. My grandfather sold out because his moral strictures forbade him being in business with a divorced man. The divorced man died years later with vast wealth. In the 1920s grandfather owned a considerable share of a group that purchased 57,000 acres of property with more than ten miles of beach of what is now Myrtle Beach, South Carolina. Unfortunately all was lost in the big crash the year I was born.

Grandfather Pope loved selling and his proudest achievement was selling the first solid boxcar load of bubble gum. Bubble gum at that time was sold in glass jars and there weren't enough glass jars to fill the order. He went all over the country rounding up glass jars. I can't imagine what they did with all that bubble gum. Perhaps whoever bought it still has some.

Sometime around 1934 my father went to Louisville Kentucky. There he visited the headquarters of the Grocer's Baking Company, a chain of commercial bread bakeries. Somehow he got in to see the president and persuaded him to hire him to run one of their bakeries. He not only got the job but they sent him to the American Baking Institute in Chicago.

Gangsters were busy spraying the streets of Chicago with Tommy gun bullets

This was at the time when Al Capon and the other gangsters were busy spraying the streets of Chicago with Tommy gun bullets. My mother was afraid that I would get sprayed so I was left with my grandparents for safe keeping while my parents went to Chicago.

Since I was the first grandchild, they all doted on me and both sides wanted me to stay with them. A compromise was worked out whereby my time with them was divided. My grandfather Pope had many books including a set of encyclopedias with lots of pictures and my grandfather was good at explaining them to me. The part I didn't like was all the instructions my grandmother gave me on how to behave like a proper gentleman. They came in handy later in life but I didn't like it at the time.

The time spent on the wrong side of the tracks with my Hunt grandparents was a lot more fun. They didn't correct my grammar and I had a teenage uncle who had a job driving a delivery truck. He sometimes took me, along with his girl friend, on his deliveries. He could only afford to buy one cigarette at a time but he also managed to buy me a stick of chewing gum. This was during the great depression. Many people could often afford only one cigarette or one stick of gum.

My grandparents had a barn in back of the house like a lot of city dwellers at the time. An old black man who was traveling around came and slept in the barn for a while. A plate of food was always set out for him on the back porch at every meal.

He was too old to do anything but sit around and whittle away on a stick. He was the first black man I had ever known and I was surprised when he told me his last name— Hunt.

I asked my grandmother Hunt who he was and why he was there. She told me that before the War Between The States the Hunts had owned a big plantation. He had been a slave on the plantation. She told me slaves often took the last names of their owners and that it was our obligation to help former slaves of the family.

For some reason black people addressed older white men as "Captain" and white people addressed older black men as "Uncle."

I was especially fond of both my grandfathers. One highlight of my youth was being taken by my Hunt grandfather on a ride in the caboose of a freight train. The thing I remember best about that event in my young life was the delicious country ham biscuits we ate in the train's caboose.

I was transported back and forth in time with each of my grandparents. My Grandfather Pope would always stop at a store about halfway and treat us both to a Coke. The Cokes in those days gave you a real zing especially on a hot day. They were loaded with caffeine and are rumored to have contained a small amount of cocaine.

A pen sketch of Grandfather Pope by a newspaper artist

My parents came back from Chicago and my father took up his new job as the production boss of the Honey Krust bakery in Johnson City Tennessee. Dad had a lot of employees, most of whom were older than he was. He was certain that he could lick any of them in a fight. He was a tough but fair boss and totally dedicated to his job.

He earned the respect of his men when he rescued, at the risk of his own life, a street repair man. A fire pot that was used as a warning in those days exploded outside the bakery. One of the repair men was on fire, running away in a panic. My father ripped off his own shirt as he threw the man down. He used his shirt to smother the fire.

Bread that was not sold after a day or two was picked up by the delivery men and replaced with fresh bread though the bread was perfectly good. My father would not let it go to waste even at the risk of hurting sales. There were many people out of work and hungry. Every Saturday morning after all the returned bread was in he handed it out free to all who wanted it. I remember seeing people lined up to receive his free bread. We, of course got our bread free, but Dad insisted that we eat the same returned bread as the people in line.

One incident I remember that enraged my father was my ordering an ice cream cone during a terrible blizzard. Drug stores sold ice cream in the 1930s and they made free deliveries. I had acquired a nickel, the price of an ice cream cone and I had seen my parents use the phone. I decided, oblivious to the blizzard raging outside, that I required an ice cream cone. I phoned in my order, which I am sure dumbfounded the people in the drugstore. Some poor soul trudged through the snow and delivered it. My father was furious, and with a very sore behind I had to beg the drugstore's forgiveness.

An incident that enraged my mother was an occasion when she had baked some lemon meringue pies. They were for her guests. It was her turn to entertain her bridge club but the pies were too much of an enticement to be ignored. I carefully lifted up the meringue and ate the pie underneath. In order to delay my mother's discovery of my eating her pies, I made matters worse by carefully arranging the meringue topping on the pies to conceal my crime.

My sister, Dee, with me on Pine Street

When she went to serve her pies my mother became livid. Her

fury would be hard to overestimate. I'm sure if she had killed me, a jury would have let her go.

I always loved learning but I hated school. However I had motivation for going. I needed to add speech to the comics I created. At first I covered flattened brown paper bags with mute drawings. I was proud when my parents showed my drawings to their friends, my childish drawings were very crude but they were my passion.

When I entered the first grade I would take a five cent composition book and turn it into a comic book. Then I would sell it for another five cents. That nickel would purchase another composition book to convert into a yet another crude comic book. I had invented perpetual motion.

This was a solution for the procurement of bound paper but it wasn't perfect. Composition books were lined and I hated to have thin blue lines messing up my creations.

It was in the first grade at the South Side Grammar School that I met the first love of my life. The five-year-old Aphrodite was named Annette Marshall. Her name rolled off my tongue like a sonnet.

Annette was the cause of my father being ashamed of me. He came home one day when Annette was chasing me around the house with a bug. I hated bugs and wouldn't touch them, My father thought it was disgraceful for a boy to be afraid of a girl with a bug.

I redeemed myself a little later when I beat a slightly older boy in a fight. He hit me with a toy rake and I came into the house crying. My father ordered me to go back out and give him a thrashing. I was more afraid of shaming my father than I was of the bully. So I went out and floored him. He never bothered me again.

In Johnson City we lived on Maple Street, then we moved to Pine Street, then Poplar Street and finally we lived on Locust Street. My family seemed to be fond of moving and the founding fathers of Johnson City seemed to be fond of trees.

My allowance at this time was fifteen cents a week. Two thirds of this sum had to go for a movie on Saturday morning. Each Saturday morning the big attraction at the Ritz Theater was *The Mickey Mouse Club*. An adult-sized Mickey Mouse would appear on stage in person and greet all the kids. This would be followed by a short film, then an animated cartoon, chapter ten of *The Hidden Empire*, next perhaps a newsreel, and then usually a cowboy movie.

My pals and I rated movies by how much shooting they contained. The more the better. Also the less love stuff the better. We liked it when something happened at the end like the horse's head coming between the hero and the heroine to prevent a kiss.

My special peeve was singing in a cowboy movie. I didn't like Gene Autry and later Roy Rogers because they were always singing some sappy song. The most detested was a group called *The Sons Of The Pioneers*. As far as I was concerned they ruined a great many westerns with their saccharin singing.

The remaining third of my allowance presented me with a serious dilemma. There were hard choices to be made. Five cents would purchase a heaping ice cream cone or a large delicious Hershey Almond Bar. If the pangs of hunger could be denied a handsome hand painted warrior could be enlisted in my lead soldier army.

The brave little lead lads that could be purchased in the five and dime stores were hollow. The hole at the top of their little noggins was concealed by a small helmet. The same nickel that recruited one soldier could recruit five helmet-less lads from a store that sold used items.

It was difficult to take soldiers with holes in their heads into battle, but recruiting an army at five cents a piece was difficult. A solution came to me like a bolt out of the blue. Acorns!

I pulled the nuts out of acorns and the remaining caps fit perfectly onto the heads of my wee warriors. My lead army was now invincible!

Soda bottle caps presented me with the opportunity if I was alone on a rainy day to command vast armies in battle on top of blanket topography. A blanket loosely thrown on the floor produced marvelous mountain ranges and valleys in its folds. And bottle caps were readily available for free in the boxes under the soda bottle openers in the stores.

Caps were usually the evil soldiers because they were the most numerous. Caps from the least popular drinks supplied the officers and the cavalry, etc.

The outcome of battles was decided by jumbling up the caps. The upside down ones were kaput.

Great naval battles were fought in the bays and inlets among islands and peninsulas that existed in the Persian pattern of the rug on our living room floor.

Matchsticks broken into the appropriate lengths magically became battleships, cruisers and destroyers. My naval wars were frequently abruptly ended when my mother entered the room and found me playing with matches.

Outdoor activities were organized by me and my friends. Back then there were no organized activities such as Little League Baseball. We just got together and chose up teams and played on a vacant lot. It was a good learning experience because we learned to negotiate and to compromise while trying to equalize the teams.

During the depression we didn't have many toy rifles or machine guns. In our war or cowboy games, a stick and our imagination did just fine.

As the happy years of grammar school passed I made some good friends and fortunate acquaintances. The father of one of my friends was a candy distributor and thus was a supplier of some sugary treats. Another friend's father worked for a magazine distributor and he kept us supplied with coverless comic books. Comic books were sold on consignment and after a certain date the covers of the unsold comic books were torn off and returned for a rebate. And my dads bakery, in addition to bread, produced mouth watering pies, cakes and donuts. We had it made!

My father hated Hitler and the Nazis. I remember him arguing with people who admired Hitler. They said Hitler was great because he had put people back to work. There were a lot of people in a little town near Johnson City who belonged to the German American Bund. There was a German owned rayon factory there that was the principle employer.

I vividly remember my family huddled around our big Zenith radio and listening to the news that Germany had invaded Poland. My family, along with most Americans, was outraged by Hitler's brutal Nazi

Nazi Stuka dive bombers
rained death down on Poland

war machine once again smashing into a smaller peaceful country.

Probably the greatest American hero of the early twenty century was Charles Lindbergh. He had become sympathetic to the Nazis and though I was too young for politics, I felt betrayed by him. I held a little ceremony and poured yellow paint on a book of his that we had.

It would be unfair if I did not point out that he later made a great contribution to our war effort. He taught our aviators how to stretch out the range of their aircraft by manipulating their engine revolutions, and his wife, Ann Marrow Lindbergh, was a great lady.

Soon after the outbreak of war in Europe we moved out into the country to Boone's Creek. My father bought some land where Boone's Creek entered the Watauga River for seventy-five dollars. The land was covered with red cedar trees. My father cleared the land for a house. Some of the trees were taken to a saw mill and cut up for lumber. He then built a house from the lumber. I always felt like I was living in a big cedar closet because that's the way it smelled.

Dad even made all the metal hinges and door latches. He hauled all the rocks for the foundation and for the big chimney and then he cemented them into place. He did all this without neglecting his full-time job and he even had to commute to the site.

He was instrumental in getting electricity run to Boone's Creek under a government program. This enabled us to have modern plumbing and he piped and pumped water from a nearby spring to the house. We were the only family in the area to have a house with modern plumbing.

Our nearest neighbor lived on top of a hill and the poor mother of the family regularly carried two buckets of water up the hill. The buckets hung from a wooden yoke around her neck.

After we moved into the house my father decided to dam up the creek to build a swimming pool. We had to construct rock walls around the soon to be pool. I was required to help. My father loved hard physical labor, but not me. He had to endure much moaning and groaning and complaining from me before the job was done.

I must confess that I did enjoy swimming in it and I remember standing by the pool on the Sunday in December when I heard that the Japanese had attacked Pearl Harbor.

War

This was a pen and ink drawing with a color overlay

I was twelve years old in 1941 and my father decided that we must be prepared to defend our country. The preparation consisted of rifle practice. Dad and I would get up on the top of a bluff over a bend in the river near our house. Trees down below overhung the river and they left only a small gap in our view of the river as the current swept by the near bank. My mother, stationed a distance up the river, would randomly throw in old light bulbs salvaged from the bakery at random. We had to rapidly take aim and fire our .22 caliber rifles to pop them as they briefly appeared in the gap. I learned how to allow for windage and how to aim just a hair in front of a rapidly moving target. When I later was in the Marine Corps,

I won a medal for sharp shooting due I am sure to my early training.

People did a lot of walking during the war. Gas was severely rationed, not so much to save gasoline, but mostly to save tires. The United States produced lots of gasoline but no rubber. The tires back then were almost all rubber. We didn't have synthetic rubber and the Japanese had captured all but about eight percent of the world's rubber sources. Only police and emergency vehicles could get tires.

When our tires wore out my father purchased an old Model A Ford because it had some tires on it that had a little wear left on them.

I was standing on its running board while it was descending a wet muddy road. It slipped into a ditch and dragged me down a barbed wire fence. I felt like I had been flayed. My entire chest was a big bloody mess. My father lay me on a table and with the admonition "take it like a

Our Model A

man, son" produced a towel and a huge bottle of iodine. He doused and swabbed me with the iodine. The pain was awful but it was the right thing to do.

Boone's Creek Junior High School was many miles away. It was necessary for me to rise long before dawn and walk a mile or more to the bus stop. There were very few buses and when we got to school there was a long wait before classes could begin. The same bus had to make another trip to pick up more kids before the whole student body was assembled.

Most of the children were very poor. Farm wages in the area were ten cents an hour or half the crop if they share cropped. All the kids were white, not because of segregation, but because I think no blacks or other races lived in Boone's Creek. It was a proud boast of most of the kids that they were part Indian. I don't know whether they were or not.

Text books had to be purchased and they were used over and over. They were usually well cared for since their condition was graded and they were priced by the teacher at the end of the year. The money from the previous year's books was most often applied to the next year's text books.

Probably because of the increasing difficulty of commuting to work in wartime the family moved back to Johnson City. I am sure this made my mother happy because she could get back with her bridge club.

We had been back in Johnson City for only a few months when my father was drafted into the army. He might have been able to get a deferment because of his age, but he felt that it was his duty to go. My mother was not happy about this, but my father was stubborn and very patriotic. Also, I think being the super macho man that he was he couldn't imagine a war going on without his being in it.

Dad's dreams of military glory were frustrated. The army decided that he would better fill its needs by helping run a school for bakers at Fort Bragg.

Mother, my sister, my young

A pen and ink drawing of my father from a photograph

CONFESSIONS OF A MADMAN   22

brother, and I moved back to Greenville South Carolina to be with our extended family. Our lifestyle was greatly diminished because we had to live off of my father's army pay and our savings. My mother was too proud to accept any money from the grandparents although they managed to help in other ways.

I was walking with crutches and my leg was in a cast when we arrived in our new home. I had split my lower right leg bone playing football during our final days in Johnson City.

Greenville High School was one of the newest, biggest and grandest schools in the state of South Carolina. It was very intimidating to me as new arrival on crutches. To make matters worse I couldn't carry my books. I had to rely on the help of perfect strangers. Back in Johnson City the kids knew that I was a temporary cripple but here I thought that they believed that I was crippled for life.

I felt like an outcast, but my imagination came to my rescue. My boyhood passion for writing and drawing adventure comic strips occupied most of my spare time.

Creating characters, putting words in their mouths and determining their fates is as close to creating life that a mere mortal can come.

Writers can come close. They can plant pictures in your mind, but the actual visual element is missing. Artists can produce the visual, but alas the rest of the elements are missing. Movie directors can make wonderful movies combining all the elements, but theirs is a collaborative effort with a number of people.

Only the humble cartoonist can play God!

Poor remnants are all that have survived of my many happy years of breathing life into heroes and villains. They are the last of Rocky O'Riley. I had to abandon him in the tinder clutches of the evil Japs. This was due to my getting a job decorating store windows after school. Also I became

My cartoons were drawn in pencil before they were rendered in India Ink. For some reason I used the pen name "Les Scott."

This was a later cartoon "inked in." I was now using my real name.

the cartoonist for my high school newspaper and I had to do at least a bare minimum of school work.

Now that I am in my dotage I get a kick out of reading the dialog of those old strips. What must have gone through my fifteen year old mind?

Les Scott was one of my pen names, I must have thought it sounded more important than Miller Pope.

I used colored inks to color the strips. It would not go on smooth and flat like the color in real comics in the paper. That color was added with a separation technique unavailable to a teenager.

It is amusing to note that I included an ad for war bonds and Corp. 1944 by JMP Service Inc. in many of the strips. Stuff like this was on the real strips.

One of my classes in school was in commercial art. Anyone who knew of my love of drawing would think that I would have taken to it eagerly. They would have been wrong because I thought the teacher was a jerk.

The state was having a high school art contest. I wanted to submit some of my cartoons. He threw them down on his desk and pronounced them trash. I pronounced him to be an idiot and he pronounced me the recipient of an F.

No doubt he was somewhat less than pleased when the journalism teacher asked me to do an editorial type cartoon for each issue of the national prizewinning school newspaper. I don't know how she knew about my stuff. I wasn't in her class but I accepted with pleasure. It was a joy to see something I did in print. I also wanted to rub my art teacher's nose in it. I don't remember how I ever came up with ideas for these cartoons but somehow I did. It is much easier to be negative in a political type cartoon than positive. It was very difficult to comment on school affairs without offending the faculty. I learned later that my cartoons were rerun in the school paper in following years.

My grades in school had begun a precipitous slide downhill from A pluses in junior high to barely passing in most classes and an F in one. The one class in which I excelled was a two hour class called historyture. History and literature were taught together and I loved them both.

I sat in the front row and I loved to give reports and make comments. The teacher took me out of the room on more than one occasion and asked me to let the other students talk.

As for algebra and some of the other subjects, I didn't see how they would benefit me in what I wanted to do in life. I must confess that my limited knowledge of English and Latin has come in handy.

Social life at Greenville High was controlled by fraternities and sororities and they were very snobbish and exclusive. Someone like me from the outside and without access to an automobile would never achieve peer popularity or be invited to their dances and other social events.

My solution to this dilemma was to create a fraternity. I had formed a friendship with a couple of bright fellow students but when I broached the idea, they told me it couldn't be done. They said a new fraternity had not been created in living memory. The existing fraternities and sororities would never accept us or invite us to their social functions.

I told my friends that I had a plan and that I was sure that it would work. They bought into my idea and we went to work.

My idea was that if we wanted to form a new organization to take on old, exclusive, entrenched society we could not appear to be apologetic. We had to come on strong and appear to be big and bad. We had to start in strict secrecy with only a tiny cadre of dedicated friends. Then expand at a measured pace but only when we had our ducks in a row.

The only way I knew to be big and bad was to appear to be part of some vast semi secret fraternity. I thought up the word "Chevalierian" inspired by the French word for a knight, chevalier. I wanted a name that couldn't be found in the dictionary and so I made one up. To make the name sound even more important, I came up with *The Royal Order Of The Chevalerian*.

Naming the president, "The Chancellor" and the treasurer "The Chancellor of the Exchequer," and coming up with an oath, bylaws and such nonsense as a secret handshake, completed the hogwash.

One of our little group aspired to be a lawyer and he helped us to be chartered as a legal eleemosynary corporation. That way if anyone tried to look us up to see if we were legit they would find that we were. He offered us an added bonus in that his basement had a large recreation room. It contained a massive oaken table and some equally massive carved high backed chairs.

We arranged the chairs for the officers to sit facing outward from behind the big table. I had designed a truly impressive coat of arms for our fraternity and I painted it on a huge sheet of sign board. Then it was mounted on the wall behind the Chancellor's chair. All this combined with a careful adjustment of the lighting, presented a most impressive and somewhat intimidating presence.

One of our charter members was the son of the owner of a jewelry store. He had some very important looking fraternity pins and keys made in gold and silver from my design.

As we secretly grew in measured steps we chose our applicants carefully. We covertly recruited many outstanding members of the junior high graduating class who were desired by the old entrenched fraternities.

When our membership grew to the desired peak and our treasury would stand it, we burst forth in a blaze of glory. We hired a big name band and put on a dance in the finest hotel ballroom in town complete with a mirrored glass ball.

The Chevalerian key

After that, in all the following years, *The Royal Order Of The Chevalierian* members were invited to all the parties and dances held by all the other fraternities and sororities.

My social life was now taken care of, but I still did not like going to school. A new program was initiated by the school board. It allowed kids who wanted to get a job to get out of school at two p.m. each day. I eagerly jumped on the opportunity.

The war had drained the nation of manpower and it was not difficult to find employment. I got a job at Greenville's largest department store as an assistant window decorator. After a short time the widow decorator was drafted. Summer had arrived and I could work full time so the management promoted me to window decorator. After that I received other promotions and at the tender age of sixteen I was the advertising manager.

The store manager told me that I had a promising future with their company but I had other plans for my future.

The armed forces of the United States had swelled to more than twelve million. The war in Europe was almost over and the army probably decided they had trained enough bakers. That, and my fathers age and family obligations, allowed him to be honorably discharged before the war had ended.

Dad wanted to open his own bakery in Greenville but an old friend of his father, my grandfather, owned a large bread bakery in Asheville, North Carolina. It was having some kind of trouble. My father was asked to take it over and straighten it out.

My father agreed to help and since this would take a matter of months, my family moved to Asheville. I went along, but I missed all my friends at Greenville High and after few months in Asheville my parents let me move back to Greenville and live with my grandparents.

Other than all my friends the best thing about moving back was that Greenville High was in South Carolina. In South Carolina you could graduate from high school after only eleven grades. This was the only state that had only eleven grades. I made it just in time because the following year South Carolina went to twelve years just like every other state. Boy, was I ever lucky!

After viewing a movie named *Wake Island* about the valiant defense of the little island from a Japanese invasion, I vowed to join the United States Marine Corps. I wanted to defend our country just as soon as I became seventeen years old. You had to be at least eighteen to serve in the army but for some reason you could be in the United States Marine Corps at seventeen. Parental permission was required at that tender age. Knowing my father's macho warrior instinct I knew that would not be a very serious impediment.

The Corps

Soon after my birthday I enlisted in the Corps. The Japanese had just surrendered but the peace treaty had not been signed, which made me an official veteran of WWII and entitled me to all the benefits of a real veteran.

The Marines were in a little war in North China to rescue American Missionaries and other Americans and foreign nationals from the tender mercies of the Chinese communists. The recruiting sergeant promised that I would be sent there. Such was my foolish enthusiasm for military glory.

The realization that I was not cut out for serious soldering was almost immediate upon my arrival at Parris Island Boot Camp. I quickly understood that the function of the two drill instructors into whose charge I had been entrusted was very simple. It was to make my life as miserable and uncomfortable as possible. In this task they succeeded admirably.

I had meekly asked the D.I. if it was true that we would be awakened at five a.m. each morning? He snarled back "shit bird you'll be sweating at five a.m." Reveille was at four a.m!

The platoon was made up, it seemed to me, mostly of a lot of former gang members from the streets of Philadelphia. It would be an understatement to say that I was not popular with them.

After thirteen weeks of constant misery with only the exception of fifteen minutes a day to write letters and one hour on Sundays for church, the hell finally ended. The number of people in our platoon had greatly diminished from the number in the beginning. A lot of members of our original platoon were given discharges because they couldn't make it through.

In the rifle pits in Boot Camp

Only one thing kept be going and that was the shame that I knew that my father would feel if I failed. Pride is a powerful motivation and I must confess that I felt good when I could pin the Marine Corps globe and eagle on my cap and become a member of the Corps. Boots ranked in the same category as prisoners in the brig and could not wear the Marine Corps emblem.

After a couple of weeks at Camp Lejune North Carolina the whole platoon was sent to the Charles Town Massachusetts Naval Shipyard as a part of the Marine guard battalion. So much for duty in China!

It was in my

bunk on the troop train en route to Boston that I made a vow to myself. I told myself that this was not the proper way to travel. In the future I would not require luxury but I would have minimum standards. When I had any choice I would need at least a clean private room and a private bathroom or I would stay home.

The time spent on guard duty at the naval base was pure unrelenting boredom and for me almost anything is better than being bored to death. Fortunately my time spent with the guard battalion only lasted a very few weeks.

My time at the shipyard started out with a great disappointment because a lot of my old platoon members were promoted to private first class. They were all selected out of those in the first part of the alphabet and Pope was in the last half. I didn't think that was fair but that's the way it was. Then suddenly out of the blue I was promoted to corporal without ever having been a private first class.

I was transferred out of the guard battalion and assigned to Admiral Richard L. Deyo, the commandant of the First Naval District of The United States as his head orderly. This meant I was "in the flag" of a very big grand honcho admiral with my own little command because his other orderlies were under me.

Since I was "in the flag" I didn't have to stand any inspections or have much to do with the guard battalion. I did however continue to live in the Marine barracks and eat in the mess hall.

In the Marine Corps easy, pleasant, cushy jobs are called "rackets" and I had fallen into one of the very best. I was stationed at the admirals official residence on the base. The Charles Town Naval Shipyard was the oldest naval base in the country and the admirals' house sat up on a hill amidst a beautiful landscape. The big house as I remember had been designed back in the early days of our country by one of the nation's top architects. The admiral lived in a grand military style with several stewards, a gardener, a chauffeur, and we orderlies. He was frequently serenaded by the base band and when he entered and left the base his flag was run up and down to signify his presence or absence.

My job was very easy in fact, I did almost nothing. During my four hours on duty, two days out of three I read, drew and walked around the grounds. Admiral Deyo had a wife and daughter but they were up in Bar Harbor Maine almost all the time. Admiral Deyo had his office in Boston rather than on the base so most of the time I had the run of the place to myself. When the admiral left his office in Boston the Marines on duty there would call me and when he entered through the main gate the Marines on guard there would call me. I would see his flag go up the pole on the U.S.F. Constitution. I would then push a little button so that a naval steward could come down and carry his brief case because carrying a officer's brief case would be considered an act of servitude. Marines don't perform acts of servitude. They do come to attention clicking their heels and saluting smartly when an admiral arrives. That's about all I did.

The only exception to this was on one occasion when part of the fleet was in and Admiral Deyo spotted a sailor walking in the distance without his cap on properly. He ordered me to ascertain what ship the sailor was from. He didn't want to know what the sailor's name was, just the name of his ship. The poor captain of the ship was reamed out for allowing a member of his crew to be improperly dressed. Of course ship's captains can't watch every member of their crew at all times but that's the way it works.

Immediately after, the captain of that ship took drastic steps to see that his crew shaped up. He stationed one of his ships' officers with the Marine guards on every gate for every watch. I am sure those officers would rather have been at liberty in town but they were given a strong incentive to help him see that every one of their ship's crew looked sharp!

I had a radio in my little office and I have since a very early age loved classical music. The admiral heard my music and since he too loved classical music and was often at the house alone, we struck up a friendship. When he also discovered that we shared a passion for history he often asked me to walk with him. Of course his lofty rank and the fact that I was only a peep squeak teenager of seventeen prevented a buddy, buddy relationship but I believe he was fond of me and he sometimes gave me tickets to the Boston Symphony and the Boston Pops that he couldn't use.

Once in a while I received tickets distributed to service men by the U.S.O. to a box at the baseball stadium to watch big league baseball. I played baseball as a kid but I would have had to be paid to watch someone else play. The tickets however were treasured by almost everyone else on the base and could be traded for favors. The mess sergeant for instance was happy to trade all sorts of special culinary delights for a ticket.

As a member of the flag it would require a higher ranking officer than Admiral Deyo to transfer me and that would require a lot of stars. So I felt that I would remain in my soft, fur-lined racket as long as I didn't do anything terrible.

One day much to my complete surprise, that "lot of stars," four to be exact, appeared out of the blue. I was ordered by the Commandant of The US Marine Corps to turn in my weapon and to report to the *Leatherneck Magazine* on Pennsylvania Avenue in Washington DC for duty on the magazine's staff.

The name Leatherneck refers to the early days of the Corps when Marines on wooden sailing ships fired from the rigging and repelled boarders. Their uniform of that time had a neck made of leather for protection from saber thrusts. Sailors and other people started calling Marines leathernecks.

The staff of the *Leatherneck* was included in Headquarters Battalion of Headquarters Marine Corps. It was a catch all organization for all the groups that the Corps didn't know what else to do with. We were the one and only battalion in the whole Marine Corps with no weapons for some reason.

It must have been somewhat unusual for a Marine general to transfer an admiral's orderly away from the admiral. I never knew why or how this happened but I was told that some sergeant (I never found out who) sent some of my drawings to a friend at the *Leatherneck*. It just happened that they were scouring the Corps for an artist. As luck would have it, one of the illustrators on the staff was painting a portrait of the commandant and I think they asked him to sign a transfer. I doubt he knew that I was attached to a flag officer and thought that it was just a routine transfer.

At any rate, I happily got rid of the responsibility of keeping my rifle clean and rust free and I reported as ordered to the magazine in Washington. The guys at the *Leatherneck* welcomed me aboard and informed me that I was "on subsistence" which meant that I received a check to pay for my rent and meals. What I did with it was up to me. They recommended a little hotel within walking distance and helped me get situated. I don't remember the name of the hotel except that it had a French name. The building housing the *Leatherneck* was just a few blocks from the White House and my hotel was on the other side. I remember seeing President Harry Truman out on a morning stroll. This was no doubt before terrorists had tried to break into the Blair House and assassinate him. At the time he was living in The Blair House, across the street from The White House because the interior of the White House was being gutted and completely rebuilt.

The leg of a piano President Truman was playing had fallen through the floor such was the sad condition of our nation's house at the time. This was the final straw and the decision was made to completely rebuild the old building. Everything was torn out of the inside right up to the bare walls and right down to the dirt floor and completely rebuilt.

This was the second time the entire inside of the White House had been rebuilt. The first time was just after it had been burned by the British in 1814. Washington had been captured in the War of 1812. Before then it had not been called the White House because it was a gray stone color just like the building in Ireland that inspired its design. The white paint applied to cover the burn marks gave it its present appearance and name.

Blair House was used to house foreign dignitaries when they were visiting the United States but was used to house the first family during the reconstruction of the White House.

During the war some of our truly great illustrators such as Tom Lovell and John Clymer had served on the staff. From their example I learned perhaps more than I could have ever learned in art school. I never really went to art school and had really never painted anything other than the coat of arms for our high school fraternity. I had aspired to be an adventure cartoonist in the mold of Milton Caniff, the creator of *Terry and the Pirates* and later, *Steve Canyon*, or Alex Raymond the creator of *Flash Gordon*. My strong point was drawing done with pencil, India ink and colored inks. But the magazine needed illustrations, not cartoons, even if the cartoons were realistic. They had a good humorous cartoonist and that was the only kind of cartoons needed.

I acquired a book entitled *Creative Illustration* by Andrew Loomis and studied it religiously. My first illustration was based on the principles of composition and technique gleaned from that wonderful book. The art director of the *Leatherneck* was very pleased with my first painting. I still have it and the book.

I spent all the rest of my time in the Marine Corps on the magazine's staff. While I was working there I studied figure drawing some

My first illustration

nights at the Corcoran School of Art in Washington.

The editorial staff of The Leatherneck was what may have been the most loosely controlled outfit in the entire Corps. Everyone liked their job and was so motivated to get published that they were eager to come to work and get the job done. The big brass pretty much left us alone, maybe because they didn't understand how a creative engine worked. All we were required to do was show up in a neat uniform with shined shoes and a haircut once every other week and get on a bus. The bus would transport us out to Arlington, Virginia. There we would line up for a brief inspection after which we would file through the office of Company D and receive our pay. We then returned to the *Leatherneck* and went our merry way.

Company D of Headquarters Battalion, Headquarters Marine Corps consisted of nothing more than a company commander and a sergeant and clerk or two. Their job was to pay and keep the records of odd ball Marine groups.

The Marine Corps would launch sudden and surprise inspections by a group of colonels on Marine posts. These were called A&I inspections. Their purpose was to keep the post commanders on their toes and they inspired fear in commanding officers.

The magazine could not have properly functioned as it did if it had functioned as military organizations normally did. For instance, a gunnery sergeant might be a writer, and the editor a private who was a great editor but had been busted down to private because of a drunken brawl. The writer would need to take his instructions from someone whom he outranked. This was taken care of by not wearing our rank on the loose fitting comfortable fatigue uniforms we usually wore while in the building. They concealed the civilian clothes we often had on underneath. We were free to wear civilian clothes while not on duty but working at the magazine was considered on duty.

One day out of the blue the A&I colonels descended on the *Leatherneck*. Panic ensued because we knew that gung ho Marine colonels who chewed battleships and spit nails would not be sympathetic to creative needs. They would flay Major Campbell, our commander, alive and he was a nice guy.

Fortunately they started the inspection downstairs with the guys in circulation who were regular gung ho types. A hurried trip out a back door procured a sizable quantity of stripes. They were hurriedly attached with rubber cement. In many cases they weren't the correct rank, but it worked. The big brass looked around and saw everyone working diligently. Everything looked perfectly normal and none of the stripes fell off. They left after a brief look around to everyone's relief. They probably didn't understand what we were doing anyway.

During my sojourn in the nation's capital I was fortunate to have an aunt and uncle who lived nearby who were of a very elevated status in Washington society. My father's oldest sister had been a very high official in the American Red Cross during the war and her husband was an important scientist and the president of the American Entomological Society. He was also a member of the Cosmos Club, considered the most prestigious club in America. Only those who have made a major contribution to the arts or sciences arts are invited to join. Someone has to die for a new member to enter their lofty ranks.

My aunt and uncle didn't have any children so they practically adopted me. My Uncle Doyle was invited to all the big parties in the capitol and they often took me. I always wore civilian clothes, often a tuxedo, and hobnobbed with the powerful without them knowing I was merely a lowly Marine corporal.

Once while walking up the gang plank to join a cruise put on by the U.S. Department of State for delegates to the "Fifth International Conference of Tropical Medicine" we were saluted by a Marine honor guard. A couple of the guys in the honor guard recognized me. Boy were they surprised to be saluting a guy that they had been drinking beer with.

The honor guard, as were all the Marine ceremonial formations, were stationed at Eighth and I Streets. I considered this to be the worst duty in the Corps. It was or is the ultimate spit and polish post. The

Commandant lives on the post and every uniform must be perfect and all shoes must look like they are made of glass. Many of the poor guys have to stand endless stretches of guard duty.

However knowing the almost unbelievable gung ho spirit of some of my fellow Jar Heads I realized that there were some who probably liked that kind of duty.

Another State Department function stands out in my memory because I carried out a conversation with Senator Stennis of Mississippi for whom a large aircraft carrier was named, and a general who was a member of the Joint Chiefs of Staff. I was sitting at a big round table with him and some other people including of course my aunt and uncle. My uncle was from an old Mississippi family and Senator Stennis was an old and close friend of my uncle.

Most teenagers would have turned to stone amid such titans. So would I have had I not had the experience of sharing my opinions with Admiral Deyo. I had the comfort of having my peep squeak rank concealed behind black tie and cummerbund.

As the nation returned to a posture of peace the Marine Corps size and budget shrank. The magazine and staff moved out to Arlington Virginia. We moved into the Marine barracks there but we were still pretty much free to come and go. Our base in Arlington was very near Washington but not close enough for walking and I had no vehicle.

One of my close friends had a motorcycle but I had to violate the solemn vow I had made to myself. The vow about either traveling in comfort or staying home when I had a choice. Riding on the back of a motorcycle is not traveling in comfort. In winter it was an act of bone chilling misery. It is hard to believe the torture to be endured by being in front without anything to break the cold wind.

It has always been a mystery to me why millions of people love misery and suffering. Witness the millions who possess other transportation and yet choose to ride on motorcycles in winter — duck hunters who spend endless hours in cold wet duck blinds, amateur boxers who find it pleasurable to be bashed on their jaw or maybe have their nose broken, to name a few.

Of course one can find oneself in a miserable situation that was not anticipated. Such a case developed out of perhaps the most exciting caper of my life. It all started when my motorcycle buddy invited me to go flying with him. I had never been up in an airplane and the prospect was truly enticing.

My pal only had a beginner's license which restricted him to flying solo but that was no obstacle. We were both teenagers and therefore invincible. Such restrictions could be overlooked. He had rented a very basic airplane, in which we were going to fly down to Cherry Point, North Carolina. Why Cherry Point was chosen as our destination I don't remember. We could just make it there to overnight and return during the span of our three day passes. It was way outside the distance we were allowed to travel away from Washington on a pass of that duration. We were flying so we didn't worry about that.

I took a bus to the airport in Alexandria, Virginia and sneaked aboard the plane. I had to duck my head down as we took off so that the pilot would appear to be alone. Our trip down to North Carolina was pleasant and uneventful although it was exciting for a wet nosed kid like me to be on an airborne adventure. Little did I know that the truly harrowing adventure was soon to ensue.

I don't remember what we did when we arrived in North Carolina. I do remember the surprise when we woke up the next morning and looked out our hotel window. Everything was covered in ice. The trees were bent over from the ice. It hung over power lines and seemed to glisten everywhere. I have seen other freak ice storms but this was the worst I ever remember.

We hurriedly dressed and rushed to the airport. Our worst fears were verified. Our little plane was covered in ice. We had to get back because any A.W.O.L. excuses would fall on dead ears. We had violated the distance restrictions. We had to fly back no matter what. To compound our already serious predicament, everything was bathed in a fog dense enough to make the flying visibility zero.

Our little craft was made of fabric stretched over a frame. When we patted it the material flexed and the ice fell off. We had to be very careful not to tear the frail fabric so we patted it with extreme care. We were told that we were wasting our time because everything was grounded. We replied that we were just finding something to do and we realized that nothing would be allowed to take off.

We were desperate teenagers afraid of nothing except the retribution of our failing to get back in our allotted time. As soon as we had the ice off the plane we were ready to go but we didn't dare expose our cards by buying fuel. What we had would have to last. A serious problem was presented by the need for starting the motor by hand. One of us had to get in front of the aircraft and rotate the propeller and jump out of the way when it started to avoid being chewed up.

This problem, usually solved by a very experienced man swinging the prop around to start it, was solved by a couple of minutes instruction given to me by my brave buddy. He had me sit behind the controls and relied on me, a person who knew nothing about airplanes, to push the right buttons as he stood in front of the prop. He yelled "contact" for me to push the switches and after a few tries the propeller started to spin. Fortunately he was able to step aside before the whirring blade could turn him into bloody hash. He got into the pilot's seat as I moved to the seat in back.

Our efforts to start the motor had come to the attention of the airport authorities. They chased us as we taxied and took off. The problems in getting airborne were minor compared to the serious problems that now faced us.

The view out the widow was nothing but solid gray. We could see nothing and of course we had no instruments save two. We had a simple compass and we had a rough idea of the direction we should take. We also had an altimeter so we knew how high up we were. By staying just a few feet above the ground we could just make out some railroad tracks. They were going in the general direction of Alexandria so we followed them.

We risked hitting wires and other obstructions but despite some close calls the God who looks after young fools was kind to us. After what seemed like an eternity the fog began to clear up, The plane was collecting ice and getting heavy. To make matters worse the fuel gauge was approaching empty.

We spotted a field that looked fairly level and we made an extremely bumpy landing on it. A farmer eventually come along and my pilot pal went off with him in search of some fuel. My duty was to hang on to the windward wing tip and keep the plane from blowing over in the

The fuel gauge was approaching empty

strong stormy wind.

    Several times the gusts lifted me several feet above ground. Despite the thought that a slightly stronger gust might flip over the frail craft and fling me off into space, I desperately clung to the wing tip with my frozen fingers.

    To my great relief he came back with some precious fuel. It wasn't the right octane but it would have to do. After fueling and repeating our death defying starting of the engine, we bounced down field. We once again were on our way. As we took off my aerial buddy pulled on a pull out lever. It fed an extra rich mixture of the fuel to the engine to boost the take off power. As he pulled the lever out it came, trailing its wires behind it, but we were airborne.

    The fuel that we had gotten was not enough to get us all the way back and we had to land again after a while. This time we landed at a small airport. The weather had cleared and the sun was out. Everything was hunky dory except when we took off again. On this, our final leg, we had to do it without the benefit of the rich fuel mixture provided by our busted lever. The little plane barely cleared the trees at the end of the runway but we made it. The sun was shinning and we thought that we had clear sailing at last. We didn't!

A little side window blew out subjecting us to the freezing air aloft. We had to endure an arctic blast that made our return trip miserable. It also confined me to bed with a fever and an awful cold for days after we returned. We did however get back on time!

When I had been in the Marine Corps about eighteen months it was announced that anyone on a two year enlistment could have an honorable discharge by simply requesting it. Much to my surprise I decided to stay in and finish my two years. I was simply learning too much on the *Leatherneck* to leave early.

The end of my enlistment did arrive after another six months and I received a "ruptured duck" emblem to pin on my uniform for the trip home. The "duck" was really a gold eagle that proclaimed that though I was still wearing the uniform, I was a WWII veteran and a civilian once again.

I spent the rest of the summer as a beach bum drinking beer, chasing girls and playing poker almost all night at Myrtle Beach, South Carolina. At the end of the summer I enrolled at Furman University to make my Grandmother Pope happy. As an official Second World War veteran I was entitled to five years of college at Uncle Sam's expense but I didn't feel that college would further my desired career as an illustrator. I had taken a college course in advertising by mail offered by the Marine Corps Institute while I was in the service. That course was of use, but I didn't think any other courses would be of benefit.

I promised my grandmother that I would go for one year just so that I could say that I had attended college. That satisfied her somewhat. I was able to get all my classes arranged before noon. That way I could freelance in the afternoon. I didn't need anytime for homework. I didn't do any homework that didn't interest me. Since I was only going for one year. and I didn't care anything about my grades.

Furman, despite calling itself a "University" was an all male school and only had a few hundred students in those days. It was connected to a female college across town and some classes were shared.

I was pledged to Phi Kappa Phi Fraternity but I never became a brother because a C average was required and my grades were abysmal. The brothers liked me and kept me on and treated me like a full fledged brother even though my grades didn't permit my formal initiation. Gallons of moonshine were always kept cold in a tub dedicated to that purpose in the fraternity house. The Phi Kaps were a merry bunch.

The one subject that I loved and made straight A's in was history. One day I was called into the Dean's office and told that the only reason I wasn't kicked out of Furman was because the Dean at the Women's college was a cousin of my grandmothers. He added "Don't even think of coming back next year." That was okay because I wasn't coming back anyway.

Fortunately for me my timing in leaving the Corps and starting my career as a free lance illustrator was about perfect. Two advertising agencies that were both slated to grow into two of the southeast's largest agencies had just been launched. I was at hand to fulfill a fair share of their need for illustration.

So great was the need for my services that one of the agencies offered me an office free of charge. It was in their suite of rooms in the Greenville News building which was at that time the tallest building in the state. They felt that it was convenient to have me close at hand even though I was free to take on assignments from their competition.

During this time I was fortunate and excited to be able to do some full color, full page advertising illustrations that ran in the leading magazines for young women — *Glamour* and *Seventeen*. One of my models and occasional date for some of my work at this time was a very beautiful girl whom I had dated a few times in high school named Joanne.

Joanne became a major movie star and won an Oscar when she

One of my first full page, full color ads

was still young. She married another super star who was America's top female heart throb but more of that later.

At the tender age of nineteen I was a big fish in a little pond and making good money. I had just seen an advertisement for a new convertible that was one of the first radically advanced designs to emerge after the war. A decision to purchase it had just been made when I received a phone call that changed me into a little fish in a big pond.

The call was from a friend from Washington whom I had met at the Corcoran School. He asked me to go to New York City with him to seek our fortune there. My decision was instantaneous. Why not?

My grandfather Pope happened to have an old friend who lived in a fancy suite in the Vanderbilt Hotel on Park Avenue. She was going to be in Europe for several months. The kind lady was willing to rent it to us during her absence for a tiny fraction of its true worth just to have someone recommended by my grandfather look after it.

Life in the big apple started off in style. In fact, it started off with a big party the first night of our arrival. The only person I knew in New York was a guy named Gary that I had befriended when he was employed as a copy writer in one of the new agencies in Greenville. Gary was an extremely good writer and one of the wittiest people I have ever known. He later wrote a novel that was on the top of the best seller list. He was the life of any party and a lot of fun to be with. But he drank too much and he was totally wild.

I remember spending one New Year's Eve back in Greenville with Gary. The two of us spent the evening consuming a whole case of champaign. We broke a case of champaign glasses in the fire place toasting the long dead Tzar. My escapades spent with Gary form a long list.

Gary came to our splendid abode to welcome us to his city and to inspire an idea. He felt that my arrival was too major an event to go uncelebrated. He felt that a party was called for. John and I ratified his idea but we had no guest list. This impediment was overcome by simply going out on the street and inviting perfect strangers to a party. Also we called some names supplied by Gary.

The party was a big success and my arrival in the big pond was off with a bang. Fortunately my grandfather's friend's lodgings survived our frolic. I'm sure she didn't have our escapades in mind when she offered us her palatial digs.

Eventually our dwelling benefactress returned and we moved to somewhat less grand but new and comfortable quarters on Riverside Drive.

In 1949 the country was undergoing a recession. I was in a big pond starting out with no contacts. I refused to seek or even consider a regular job because I wanted to freelance. I still did a few jobs from afar for the agencies back in Greenville. This, however, became increasingly difficult. I met a beautiful young model that I had employed to pose for one of my Greenville jobs. We began a serious affair which ended one day when she came to me crying and told me we had to end it. She seemed to be terrified of something. I was never able to find out what it was although it seemed to have something to do with her family. She begged me not to investigate the reason if I loved her. I had to promise not to. I kept my word but it was a hard thing to do. I never saw her again.

Even though I was married to my wife Helen for fifty-one years and loved her completely, I can't help remembering the young model and wondering what ever happened to her. I hope that she has had a long, prosperous and happy life.

As time went by my sources of work from Greenville slowly dried up and I was unable to find new ones in the big city. My savings also went down the drain. I was broke and much too proud to let my family back home know.

I had personally paid all the rent since we had arrived in New

York relying on my roommate's word to pay me back when he got a job. He went back to Washington and got a job with the post office. After making excuse after excuse he finally admitted that he had spent all the money that he had made. That was the end of our friendship. I have never spoken to him again.

My ex friend's betrayal had left me in an enormous financial hole. I was completely broke except for a few coins. They were invested in a box of rice and a large can of tomato paste. Thus slow death by starvation was barely averted.

I received a telephone call for my ex friend. It was to inform him that he was being hired for a full time job he had applied for. He had used my samples to get the job. I could have taken it but even in the face of starvation I turned it down. I was a freelance illustrator!

There was no possibility of my continuing to pay the rent. There was only one honorable thing to do and I did it. I went to the owner and informed him that since I could not pay anymore rent I would vacate the apartment by the end of the month. The rent was paid up until then. He thanked me and voided the lease.

Shortly before my departure the decision to have a party was made by myself and a couple of friends. One of them said that a guy he knew was about to have a birthday. We decided that we would celebrate it. It was easy to have a party with no money. All you had to do was tell the people invited that it was a B.Y.O.B. party. "Bring Your Own Bottle."

I knew that there were some girls who lived in an apartment upstairs even though I had not met them. I pushed an invitation under their door.

The day of the party my power was shut off because of an unpaid bill. We were undeterred because we simply substituted candles. The party was a big success. A bunch of girls from Hunter College attended who looked beautiful in the soft candlelight.

One of the young ladies was carried away by the party spirit. She thought it to be a very witty act to open my bureau and hand out a pair of my under drawers to each new arrival. Thus my future wife, Helen, one of the girls upstairs was introduced to my underwear before she was introduced to me!

As a result of our meeting at this last party on Riverside Drive Helen and I began a life-long love affair that ended more than fifty years later with her death.

Shortly after the party I was invited upstairs to partake of some cake Helen and her two roommates had baked. The three demure young ladies were surprised by my prodigious appetite. They didn't know that I was practically starving because of my reduced circumstances. All three came from very wealthy families and poverty was unknown to them.

In order to stave off starvation for as long as possible I enrolled in a class at The Art Student's League. The only class that was open was in Reginald Marsh's class. He was a very famous painter who was the darling of many art critics. I considered his stuff to be pure crap because he couldn't draw. He had nothing to teach me. I could however get some practice drawing from a live nude model and Uncle Sam sent me seventy-five dollars a month to help me stay alive thanks to the G. I. Bill.

Helen and I started going out together although all I could afford was a beer. She had never seen the less privileged side of life let alone nude women and almost nude men posing in an art school.

Helen's was a true blue blood. Her parents were listed in the New York Social Register which proclaimed their status in the upper levels of snobbery. She had graduated from a top Ivy League Women's College. She was the direct descendent of the first governor of the Massachusetts Bay Colony and many other illustrious ancestors. Every male on both sides of her family had always gone to Princeton back into antiquity and the list goes on.

It is not hard to imagine how unhappy her parents must have been that she even knew a hick like me from the hills of Tennessee. They were probably hoping that she would wed Lord Peter something or other, whose father was chairman of the board of a major international corporation. She would have become Lady something-or-other in England. He was after Helen hot and heavy. After they would return from some of New York's most exclusive and expensive supper clubs Helen and I would go out for a beer. After a short while Helen gave lord Peter his walking papers much to her parents great distress.

The Black Hole

Somehow I heard about an extremely cheap room for rent above Kelley's Bar on Lexington Avenue just off Forty-Second Street. It was on the third floor and the stairs went straight up with no landings. It was dark and dingy with only a small window that opened to a tiny air shaft. There was a single sink that doubled as a lavatory. The room was so small that I had to climb over the bed to get to the miniature bathroom. It was straight out of a Dicken's novel. I called it "The black hole of Forty Second Street".

As diminutive and awful as the black hole was I had to share it with a roommate. Angie my fellow sufferer was a recent graduate from Harvard. He had graduated Magna cum Lauda which causes one to ask how such a mass of gray matter could wind up in a black hole? Perhaps one instance could shed a ray of light on the matter.

One day Angie came back to our dark cave and proudly showed me a "Diamond" ring that he had procured on the street for a bargain. I had to ask him if the guy also had any bridges for sale.

The end of my suffering and my life in the dim, dark, and dingy dwelling above Kelley's Bar was brought about by the Eberhardt and Faber Pencil Company. Their ad agency in New York was looking for someone to do some humorous cartoon drawings for their ads. A guy I knew who worked on that account told me about it. I knew that good humorous cartoonist were not in short supply in the city. I had never done humorous cartoons but I decided to give it a try. I made some samples and my friend took them and flashed them in front of the client. Much to my pleasant astonishment I got the assignment for supplying the art for the whole campaign.

I could now come up with the rent on vastly improved digs. As luck would have it while visiting Helen and her roommates with two of my friends in tow, Gus Heinze and Gill Crieger, I stumbled onto a fantastic abode. Helen and her roommates had moved into a new apartment on the ground floor of a white marble mansion just off of Central Park West. It had once been the home of Jessie P. Livermore who had been known before the great depression as "The boy wonder of Wall Street." The great marble entrance hall had a lot of impressive life size marble statues in it and was most impressive. Helen's apartment had been created out of the rooms beyond the hall.

As we were leaving we happened to meet Helen's landlady in the hall. I asked her if anything was available in the building. Much to my surprise she answered in the affirmative. She led us up the grand staircase from the hall and showed us a duplex apartment on the second floor. I was bowled over by it. The living room was vast and baronial. It had twelve foot stained glass windows in an alcove with a life-size marble statue of a nude girl. It also sported a fireplace and mirrors of truly epic dimensions. There was a kitchen/dining room and a bedroom on the same floor as the big living room. There was another bedroom up some stairs in the apartment. Both my buddies were eager to share the rent with me and were in a position to change their abodes.

The situation in the black hole had reached a crisis. My plumbing had reached the point of barely functioning and Kelley refused to do anything about it. I felt cheated so I felt no qualms departing without notice owing him his last month's rent.

The night of my departure was quite dramatic. Gus, one of my new roommates, possessed a huge Buick four door convertible that looked like the car that Hitler rode around in. He risked a ticket by parking it outside *Kelley's Bar* adjoining the door to the steep stairway that led up to the black hole. The door to the stairway was only a few steps from the bar entrance. Kelley sometimes stood outside the bar for a few minutes in the summer and this was summertime.

Just as we came out of the door to the street and flung the last of my belongings into Gus's mighty leviathan Kelly emerged from the bar. He realized that I was running out on him. We hastily departed drowning out Kelley's curses in the big black Buick's exhaust fumes.

At long last, I was on my way back up in the world. I received some assignments doing illustrations for a book club that appeared on the back of magazine supplements that were enclosed with Sunday newspapers.

Somehow, I don't remember how, I got connected up with Fawcette Publications penciling comic book magazine stories. Fawcette had a super hero *Captain Marvel* which actually outsold *Superman*. They were later successfully sued by *Action Comics* which owned *Superman*. They had to go out of the comic book business.

I made good money for my age penciling comic books because I got thirty-five dollars a page and I could do at least three pages a day. In 1949 and 1950 that went a long way. I just drew the pages in pencil. Someone else inked my pencils. Yet another person did the lettering and the speech balloons.

Helen begged me to stop because someone told her that it would ruin me as an illustrator. My drawing would become too stylized by the speed with which I worked. I might not have been keen to follow her advice if I had been kept doing crime stories. Fawcette changed me to penciling teen romance stories. They tried to console me by telling me that they used their best artists on these stories. I knew that was bunk. They got censored by the board set up to keep the comics pure and puritanical. I had drawn a scene of a crook breaking a bottle across the face of another crook.

For a short while I held my nose between pinched fingers and drew a few more saccharin teen romance stories but I soon quit and went back to illustration of a somewhat higher status.

I joined an art studio called The New York Artist as one of their illustrators. In those days the big studios consisted of a group of salesmen, known as representatives. A staff of employees known as "The bull pen" was under an art director. They did paste-ups and mechanicals. Lastly there were the management and accounting people. In addition to the salaried and hourly employees there were usually a group of illustrators represented by the studio. The illustrators were free to do work on their own except for the studio's accounts.

The studio provided ample space for the illustrator to work in plus all the art materials, messenger services, telephone etc. The illustrator and the studio split the money paid for the illustration jobs brought in by the studio's representatives. The studio got no money from any jobs done by the illustrators on their own.

In addition to illustrators. there were other specialists who were necessary for producing commercial art. There were

lettering men who did the special lettering for headlines by hand, these lettering styles were not available in type fonts as they are today. It was a treat to watch the skill with which the good ones performed their task. I remember watching Pete Dom, who has fonts on today's computers named after him, lettering an ad. He had to letter it directly on top of the art. The slightest slip would have meant disaster, but he did it flawlessly. Lettering was truly an art.

There were photo retouchers who mostly used the airbrush. Photo retouching is as easy as duck soup today thanks to the computer. It was not back then. Art and great skill were required. As far as I know, there was only a couple of retouchers in New York who could retouch color reversal film like kodachrome. To have it done was very expensive. The solution to retouching a color photo was to have the picture shot with color negative film and have a color print made. The print was retouched, rephotographed and reprinted. The result was not as good as that from a kodachrome but often that was the only option.

Photographers had a much more challenging job in the past before strobe lights, digital cameras and computers. The lights were so hot that perspiration on models was a problem. It presented such a problem to food photographers that mashed potatoes were used for ice-cream and drinks contained ice cubes made of glass. The foam on beer and the water running down the side of the glass had to be added by a retoucher.

The computer replaced many of the skilled people mentioned above, plus the guys who made photostats and set type. If I had my Macintosh back then I could have ruled the world.

Most of the studios were honest but I had one experience with gross dishonesty. I was told by a studio rep that if I did a great job on a finished composite of a liquor display that I would get the finished job. Composites simply called "Comps" were done to show the client what to expect in the finished job. They came in three flavors that were as they sound: rough comps, comps, and finished comps.

I was eager to get the finished job because it paid a lot of money. I busted my rear end working endless hours over an entire holiday weekend. I produced a comp that looked like a finish. After waiting several weeks to find out how it was received, I found out. I was walking by a store and to my surprise there was my comp in the form of a printed display! The rep gave me a song and dance story about it being done by someone else but he lied. I was intimately acquainted with it after having spent so much time doing it. He had sold it as the original and pocketed my money and maybe greased some palms along the way.

I was associated with a number of studios over the next several years and had happy relations with them for the most part. I also had independent art reps. For their services of selling the art, delivering it, and performing any other back and forth necessary, they received a twenty-five percent commission. Selling art was called "Flashing samples." I didn't like to do it, besides reps could tell the perspective client how wonderful you were. It was difficult to beat your own drum without exposing your egotism.

Advertising illustration was the most lucrative but editorial illustration was the most fun. Advertising illustration usually originated with a comp supplied by an agency art director that provided a map to what was desired. Editorial illustration usually began with a script and instructions as to whether it should be a halftone, a duatone or four color illustration. About the only other instruction from the art director was the amount of space allotted. Sometimes the shape and allotted placement of the title was specified.

For tax reasons magazines didn't purchase the illustration, they purchased first publication rights. After publication the art was returned. Sometimes a printer or foreign publication would buy second publication rights. This was pure gravy but the remuneration was small compared to

One of my early magazine illustrations

the first time around.

    Life in my new spacious and luxurious dwelling was pleasant. I have never had to return to a black hole. Our digs were too grand not to be shared with lesser folk. They simply cried out to be the site of truly grand merriment. We met the challenge by having a party of lofty dimensions practically every week. Our parties were all B.Y.O.B. so the booze bill was nil. All we supplied were pretzels and potato chips. We started off by inviting friends and telling them to invite all their friends. Soon we were "The party" in New York to attend. We entertained celebrities, models, beautiful call girls, and artists, actors and writers of every sort. We had one party that lasted for an entire weekend. The dregs or maybe survivors is a better word ended up out on Jones Beach on Long Island. Jones Beach had long stretches of empty beach back then. I doubt if it is like that today.

Helen, while she could party with the best of us, also loved her sleep. She usually quit the parties and went downstairs to her apartment around midnight and got her sleep but I partied on.

One day my roommates and I went to the beach at Coney Island in Brooklyn. One of my buddies spotted this extremely beautiful girl whom he recognized as *Miss Subways* sunning on the beach with a couple of girl friends. The New York subways advertising agency had put on a competition to find the most beautiful girl who used the subway. The title of *Miss Subways* was bestowed on her. Her picture was displayed in every subway car and thus she was recognizable. My roommates were bowled over by her beauty but too afraid to approach her.

Our conversation about her somehow resulted in me making them a bet that I could get a date with her. I never had a problem approaching girls so I went right over to the ladies and entered into a conversation. I have no idea what I said but it resulted in our spending the rest of the day with them. Also it led to some dates with her in the following days. She was a very innocent and unsophisticated young daughter of a devoutly religious Roman Catholic Irish Family. She lived way over in the far reaches of Brooklyn. She really didn't fit into the Bohemian lifestyle I was living and so our relationship gradually dried up.

On top of everything else Helen found out about her and was

livid. I truly loved Helen and you can't love two women at the same time. I promised to not see her again and I kept my promise. All this led to one of the things that will haunt me to my final day. A month or two passed after my last date with little *Miss Subways* and in the midst of a roaring New Year's Eve party in my apartment I was called to the phone.

I was greeted by a tearful voice. She had looked forward all this time to my taking her to our New Year's Eve Party. I had invited her many weeks back and I had assumed that she had forgotten about it. She told me that she had thought of almost nothing else the entire time even though I had not called. I felt like a total rat and I still do. I didn't think that such a beautiful creature could remain interested. I realize now that I had probably introduced her to a lifestyle that she had never experienced in the depths of Brooklyn. I only hope that her life has been a happy one.

Sometime around this time as I was walking on Fifth Avenue I heard a rapping on the inside of a glass window in a store that I was passing. Joanne, the girl I had dated back in Greenville, was rapping to gain my attention. She told me that she was living temporarily with her father across the Hudson River in New Jersey. She gave me her telephone number and asked me to call her. Joanne was beginning to make a name for herself as an actress. She had some leading parts in *Studio One* on CBS. *Studio One* was a ninety minute drama that was one of the most popular early television programs. I didn't call her because after my little affair with *Miss Subways* any contact with an old high school girl friend might get me into trouble with Helen.

I made the mistake of mentioning to my roommates that I had met Joanne and that she had given me her phone number. After being subjected to intense badgering by them I made what I know today was an unpardonable sin. I surrendered the number. She never spoke to me again even though we both lived for many years in what was for most of those years a small town, Westport, Connecticut.

My life was proceeding at a happy pace. When I was not partying I worked into the wee hours and sometimes all night. Of course this necessitated my sleeping until noon most days. One night in the wee hours Gus and I were sitting around with Gary J drinking numerous whiskey sours or some other sweet drink consumed by youth. Gary announced that he had a two week vacation starting the next day. He asked if we would like to accompany him somewhere. The suggestion was made that it might be fun to just start out immediately and follow our nose. The idea was instantly approved and we were on our way. I had only one hundred and fifty dollars in the apartment. I suggested that we each bring only an equal amount. Gary and Gus readily agreed.

Gus had a big Lincoln Continental Cabriolet. At the time this particular car was the most beautiful of all American cars. It was later selected by The Museum of

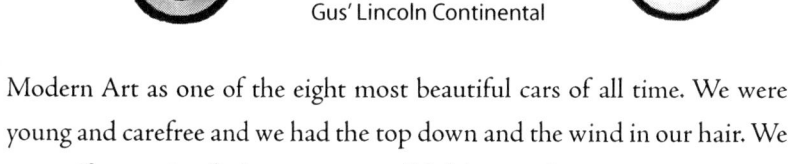

Gus' Lincoln Continental

Modern Art as one of the eight most beautiful cars of all time. We were young and carefree and we had the top down and the wind in our hair. We were off on a trip of adventure to we didn't know where.

After a few hours on the road we found ourselves stopping for snacks in a little country store in Vermont. The large type on a magazine cover proclaimed "Montreal, City of Sin." That was it! We were destinationless no more. We were off to Montreal!

As hard as we looked we didn't find any sin in Montreal but we did exhaust our meager funds. We got back without undue hunger and the ability to feed the appetite of our grand conveyance by camping out and eating cheap food. One serious impediment to easy camping was our lack of camping gear. We had only my two-year-old Marine Corps blankets, one pot, three or four knives, forks and spoons. We also had a lot of fire crackers.

We usually had a supply of firecrackers even though they were illegal. The parents of one of the girls in our crowd had a house up on a lake in Vermont. The whole crowd often piled into a couple of cars on a Friday afternoon during the summer and drove up to the lake. We got up there in time to dive into the lake as the sun was coming up. The water was always frigid but we were too young to care.

As we drove through the sleeping hamlets in the wee hours of the morning we thought dropping strings of firecrackers out of the car and arousing the populace was great sport. We were oblivious to the misdemeanor known as disturbing the peace. I'm sure the police would not have appreciated our pranks if they had caught us but they never did.

The fire crackers came in handy one night on the return leg of our failed odyssey in search of sin. We were in the depths of northwestern Maine and we had never been in a true wilderness before. It was so empty and quiet that you could hear your body functioning. We knew that it was a dwelling place for bears, moose and God knows what other creatures our minds could dream up. The night was cold and we had only two old blankets which we couldn't share if we attempted to sleep in the car. We had to use one blanket on the ground which meant we had to sleep closer to get under one blanket than heterosexual guys prefer but heterosexual guys also prefer not freezing to death.

We placed ourselves between the car and a fire that we had built and armed ourselves with firecrackers to throw into the fire if we were attacked by any big fierce varmints during the night.

Shortly before dawn the car began to shake. Something big was rubbing against it on the other side. Firecrackers went into the fire. After all the quiet the deafening noise was accompanied by a dramatic flash of light. We all jumped up and our sleep was over.

The dawn light revealed that a lot of dirt and dust had been wiped off the car all the way up the side. We never knew by what.

Shortly before our night of fright we had run into some trouble when we crossed back into the United States from Canada. We were all asked our place of birth and Gus answered honestly, Bremen Germany. He was then told he could not enter the country without proof of citizenship. Gus was a citizen but he couldn't prove it. After much worry we found in Gus's luggage something that showed that he had served in the U.S. Army. To our great relief the border guard was satisfied and we reentered the country.

Many of my male friends were drafted to serve in the Korean

A "wash drawing" (*India Ink* and water) of a Korean War illustration

War but I was exempted from the draft because I was "officially" a WWII veteran.

Helen had moved diagonally across Central Park into an apartment provided by her parents just a few doors off the park. Maybe they felt she was too near to me living in the same building. Anyway, it was a pleasant walk through the corner of the park to reach her new abode. I felt safe walking in Central Park even at night in those days.

Helen's parents had come to accept me. Helen may have given them no choice. I was exposed to the life of money and privilege which for the most part I did not enjoy. Living in a house with servants around intrudes on ones privacy. You have to be careful of your conversation and one's freedom to be spontaneous is curbed. For instance the time taken up by the cocktail hour has to be reasonably precise, as the cook has been told when to have the meal hot and ready.

Yachts might be fun for drug lords and movie moguls. I found it boring to travel on the *Roving Lady II*, Helen's father's big boat.

Helen and me on the *Roving Lady II*

I have found most boat trips boring. You can see an island in the distance and even when you are going at a pretty good clip an hour later it looks just as far away. I did enjoy being with Helen but I couldn't do much smooching with her parents around, even though it was a big boat. I remember yearning for the cocktail hour to arrive.

I did get to spend plenty of hours alone with Helen when I went out to visit her at their big house outside the city in Scarsdale, New York. Her family had a number of cars and we could take one and go off on our own. They belonged to a bunch of clubs with a lot of recreational facilities. We rarely took advantage of them except for the numerous parties. Helen loved to dance.

Helen and her family were constantly invited to big parties in big houses and I went with her.

A Tied Knot

I had saved the money to purchase the nifty sports car of my dreams but Helen and I had been together for a little more than three years. I had reached the advanced age of twenty three so I decided that it was time to pop the question. Helen had just arrived back from a trip to Texas when I performed the corny act of going down on my knees and asking for her hand. She gave me a resounding yes!

The new bride   On the way to the church   Helen's parents

Cutting the cake   Throwing the bouquet

The engagement ring was purchased with the money I had saved to buy the car and I told her that I had little money left but she didn't care. When I asked her father for her hand he assented and the wedding plans went into action.

Thank God the bride's parents pay for the wedding because our wedding must have cost a King's ransom. We had one of the country's top orchestras for the reception. We also had the best wedding photographers and what seemed like hundreds of guests. The wedding took place in a Presbyterian church in Scarsdale where Helen's father had donated the bell tower.

The reception took place at The Shenarock Shore Club on Long Island Sound in nearby Rye, New York. The wedding gifts were mountainous. When Helen died, over fifty years later, she had fine crystal still in the original box. It had never been used.

Helen had a beautiful diamond wedding ring and a boatload of silver, crystal and china. I had, however, only a little money for a honeymoon. I would not let Helen give me any money because I was taught by my family that gentlemen don't take money from women. I have never even let women go Dutch with me.

I had enough money for a week at a resort on Cape Cod and our first night while we were traveling in a hotel in Greenwich, Connecticut. While my pride and proper manners prevented me from accepting any money from Helen or her family, I did accept the loan of a new car and the loan of a lake house from Helen's uncle for our second honeymoon week.

Our marriage got off to a bad start because I didn't like the resort where we spent our first week. Breakfast which has always been my favorite meal, wasn't served after nine a.m. We never were able to get there that early. What really turned me off was the cutesy sign on the table outside the closed entrance door to the breakfast room. Coffee and Danish was left for those who didn't arise at the crack of dawn. It said "For The Little Sleepy Heads."

I didn't want anyone to know that we were honeymooners. I had asked Helen not to wear her corsage so as to not give the secret away. It was to no avail. The entire staff greeted us as honeymooners from the very start. I asked the young college girl from Boston, who was working there for the summer, how they knew. She confessed that she had told them because she had been to one of our big parties in New York.

We were asked to hang some kind of "Cutesy" corny plaque on a tree to which our children's names would be attached when we supposedly came back in future years. I had my fill of such stupid nonsense. The resort had very beautiful gardens but they did not make up for the lack of a bar. I told Helen that this place might be a good place to smell roses when we got to be seventy. At our age we were not interested in smelling roses. She readily agreed. I told the front desk that we were called back to New York on sudden notice. We checked out and resumed the honeymoon at her Uncles Hal's house on Emerald Lake in Connecticut.

Uncle Hal had recently held a big party for members of Dial Lodge, his old club at Princeton, and he had left gallons of manhattan ingredients. Rye Whiskey and Vermouth and a note welcoming us and telling us to feel free to partake of his favorite elixir. We spent the rest of our honeymoon in wedded bliss, secluded in Uncle Hal's comfortable rustic house on a beautiful lake, with a bountiful supply of Manhattans for the cocktail hour.

When we returned to Manhattan we had a brand new apartment awaiting us. It was a one bedroom, one bath apartment in a new apartment complex called Stuyvesant Town near the East River in lower Manhattan. Our little apartment also had a living room, a small kitchen and an entrance foyer. It was on an upper floor but there were elevators and it had large windows that overlooked attractive, landscaped grounds with a park like atmosphere.

Because the rents in Stuyvesant Town were so reasonable, there

A couple of book covers done soon after Helen and I were married

was a long waiting list for them. I later became aware that some strings may have been pulled because Helen's father was a friend of the chairman of the board of the giant insurance company that owned the complex.

The decor of our new digs was inspired by the great modern artist Piet Modrian. All the walls were white and the furniture was all black with touches of bright color in prints of paintings and other items by modern artists like Raul Dufy. The furniture was not really very comfortable. We later got over our extreme attachment to all the modernity. We were young and I suppose we wanted to be sophisticated.

We met another young couple who lived on our floor and we shared the cocktail hour several times a week with them. Helen had quit her job as a copy writer at Crowell Collier Publishing Company when we got married and fortunately I was able to find enough work to provide us with a decent standard of living. About nine months after our wedding our daughter Debra was born and we moved into a larger apartment with two bedrooms in the same complex.

During the early years of my career, I had been represented by several studios. The last one was a small one in which I was the only illustrator. It occupied some prime real-estate on Madison Avenue and I occupied a large room in the establishment. The studio was providing me with almost no work. I had an independent art rep who was keeping me busy. This state of affairs was great for me because an independent rep got twenty-five percent when the studio would have gotten fifty.

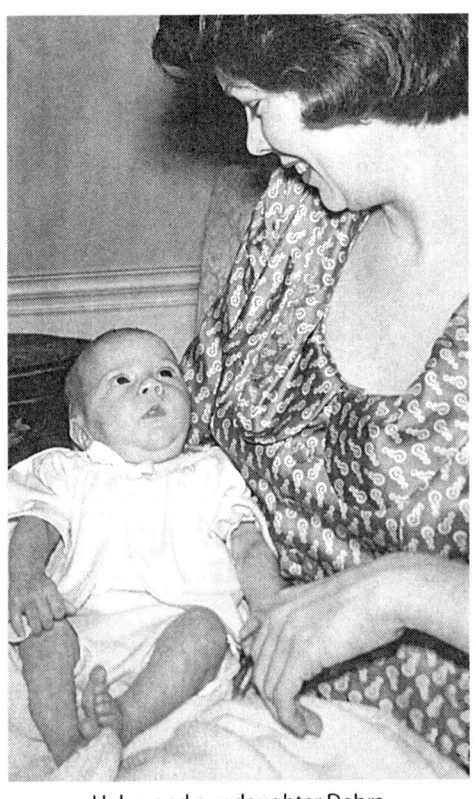

Helen and our daughter Debra

I was sitting in the old cat bird seat in my little high rent nest with them paying all the rent. I knew that this could not go on much longer. I felt that now was the time to try something that I had in the back of my mind. Why not start an advertising agency?

The studio I was currently in had a very talented young art director, Andy Morimoto. Andy was of Japanese decent and had been interned during the war with his parents, but he was as American as the Fourth of July. He was one of the most talented designers I have ever known and he was just what a good ad agency needed.

Another vital need was a good salesman. I had met William

Stringfellow through Helen. She had worked with Bud, as he was called, at Crowell Collier. I knew that he had the personality of a good salesman.

Bud and Andy had never met but somehow I talked both of them into leaving their perfectly good jobs and going into partnership in an ad agency with me. None of us had ever even worked in an advertising agency. I had taken a correspondence course in advertising. Andy and I had both done a lot of work for agencies but that was the extent of our experience.

Never the less, Stringfellow, Pope and Morimoto was given birth. The newborn babe, was up on its feet almost before it was out of the womb. A very small but well situated perch from which our new business could take flight was procured on Fifty Seventh Street between Fifth Avenue and Sixth Avenue.

The rent was very small for such a lofty location because the building in which it was located was slated for demolition. Our occupancy would cease as soon as all the property needed for a new building on the site was purchased. The lease was only month to month. It required evacuation on very short notice. Our one room was so small that we could all barely walk around at the same time.

To make our humble nest as presentable as possible we gave its ancient walls a fresh coat of paint. The paint was still wet when to our amazement Bud Stringfellow brought us our first job.

Andy and I were overjoyed that Stringfellow, Pope and Morimoto was off to such a quick start. We were knocked for a loop when Bud told us what he had promised to get the job.

All we had to do was design and produce a finished full-color comprehensive layout consisting of a number of pages for The Erie Forge and Steel Company by nine a.m. — the next morning. All we had to do was do at least a week's work overnight with no place to do it in. Bud would never have promised to do this if he had been experienced in his job. Never the less the impossible had to be done and we did it!

Andy still had his key to the studio on Madison Avenue that he and I had only left a few days before. We knew that everyone there left by five p.m. The security guards in the building knew Andy and I, and Bud would not be questioned if he entered with us. We waited across the street

The cover done for Stringfellow, Pope and Morimoto's first job

73   CONFESSIONS OF A MADMAN

until everyone left on schedule and then in we went.

Andy and I had used the time until we could get into the old studio sitting in a coffee shop laying things out on paper napkins so that the three of us were off with a bang. We worked like demons throughout the night. Just like in the movies we finished the job with only minutes to spare before we had to clear out. We made it by the skin of our teeth.

The client loved the job!

Fortune smiled on the three of us and soon we moved to much more spacious quarters just a few steps off Fifth Avenue on Forty Second Street. We now had several good employees even though we were still a very small agency. Most of our accounts were small companies but we did trade ads for some large companies.

Steady income came from a number of "House organs" (company magazines) we produced monthly for some major corporations.

Our most lucrative account was a huge international construction company. We placed full page ads in *Fortune* and other business magazines

Some of the employees of *Stringfellow, Pope and Morimoto*

for the firm. Our agency received a fifteen percent commission on the very substantial ad rates. This would have been a very sweet deal except for having to keep the ad manager for the big firm out of our shop. The ad manager was the son of the president of the firm and he was a total lush.

When he showed up he was almost always drunk. Bud would have to take him out and bar crawl with him so we could get some work done. He only appeared now and then and Bud could handle him so it wasn't too bad.

One time, fortunately only once, the ad manager showed up and Bud could not be contacted. The job of getting him out of the shop fell to me because Andy was a teetotaler. I don't remember how I managed to get rid of him. It was only after seeing the inside of a number of different bars. It was truly remarkable how he could keep standing after consuming oceans of booze.

One day a very distinguished well-dressed gentleman appeared at the agency and presented his card. It identified him as the president of The Friends Of Pompeii. He told us that the ancient city of Pompeii was slowly being destroyed by the pollution of modern air. It was the mission of his organization to take measures for its preservation. A new brochure was needed to help in this noble crusade. He wanted to employ our agency to design, produce and have it printed.

I felt that since the preservation of antiquity was indeed a worthwhile cause we should do it for his nonprofit organization as reasonably as possible. To that end I told him that he could save money on the printing by dealing with a printer directly. This would save them the usual commission we would charge for handling that part of the job. He thanked me for that advice and we got to work.

The brochure was produced to his satisfaction and sent to the printer he had engaged. Our bill was okayed by him and sent to the address of his organization in the prestigious Graybar Building. When it wasn't paid after a reasonable time we found out that the office in the Graybar Building no longer existed. He was a con man! Thank God we were not responsible for the printing. I could only feel bad for all the people he was scamming using the brochure we had produced.

Helen and I decided that it was time we had a house of our own in the suburbs. Even though I liked my partners and the guys that worked for Stringfellow, Pope and Morimoto, I missed the freelance life. I also knew that when we moved out of town I would have to commute into the city every day. I wouldn't like that.

Connecticut had the advantage of no state income tax. This made it ideal for anyone who didn't earn a salary in the city. Helen's mother and father had separated. Her mother had taken the very large house with spacious grounds and a pool they owned on Pound Ridge in New Caanan, Connecticut. She invited us to stay there as long as we liked while we looked for a house. I was very fond of Helen's mother so

My daughter Debra, Andy Morimoto and his daughter Lynn by the pool in New Canaan

A picture Helen took of me feeding little Gary

we took up her kind offer and moved in.

Our son Gary had just been born and he was allergic to regular milk just as I had been as a baby. The doctor put him on some awful soybean stuff. He would throw it up about as fast as you could get it down him. Helen kept telling the doctor that I had been on goat milk as a baby. He wouldn't listen. Helen's mother employed a nurse to help Helen and when they finally put little Gary on goat's milk he was fine.

Helen's only uncle died soon after we moved to New Caanan and we were given his car along with a house on Emerald Lake in Sherman, Connecticut. The lake house had a spectacular twenty mile view over Candlewood Lake from the rear. It also had frontage on Emerald Lake, which is about five hundred feet higher than Candlewood Lake. It would have been a great place to live but it was too far from New York City for year round living.

The place to live for an illustrator was Westport. It was the "In" place to reside. For that reason, I wanted to live some where else. My ego, was such that I rebelled against such nonsense as doing the "In" thing. Fate had other plans for me.

At a party in Greenwich, Helen and I had a conversation with one of her old school chums from Scaresdale about houses. We knew that Mary, her old buddy, was a real penny pincher. When she mentioned that she had found a house in Westport that was a "Steal," our antennas went up. Mary declared that the only problem with it. was that there were a lot of "Italians" in the neighborhood and her children would have to go to school with them.

Neither Helen nor I had ever heard of anyone having any trouble with "Italians." They were just fine with us. After all "Italians" had produced Roman civilization, Michelangelo and DeVinci. Some of these "Italians" came to number among our best friends. Mary's stupid prejudice worked

Main Street in mid-century Westport

to our advantage. We got a great buy in our first house. It also led to our good fortune in residing in Westport. Which led to making many good friends, some of our country's nicest and most talented people.

Westport was a small town but it abounded in creative people of every stripe. Famous illustrators, novelists, TV personalities, movie actors, playwrights, industrial designers and ad men practically crawled out of the woodwork. There was a top flight library with a picture reference section the likes of which few big cities could boast. There was an art supply store that rivaled the best in New York. There was a first class camera store and summer theater that was one of the best in the country. The Westport Artists was a club that was almost on a par with the Society of Illustrators and the Art Directors Club in New York.

The little town had excellent public schools, an abundance of excellent restaurants and many town-owned recreational amenities including three beaches, a yacht club and a country club. It had two railroad stations on the direct line to New York and Boston. All

Debbie and Gary were used as models for this illustration

Our "Mondrian" living room

and no state income tax made it the perfect place to live in the New York area. Helen and I owed our good fortune to ignorant prejudice.

Our new house was a split level, which had a very large recreation room in addition to the living room. The living room was furnished with our rather severe Mondrian modern furniture from our New York apartment. The big recreation room downstairs was furnished with more traditional and more comfortable furniture. The living room was seldom used. We had come to value comfort over pseudo sophistication.

The big recreation room had a fireplace which seemed to demand bookshelves on both sides and I decided to try my hand at carpentry. Westport had changed my taste in furnishings from modern to early American. The ideal dwelling in Westport was a converted barn. There were some truly magnificent ones. Old houses with wooden beams were also much desired and I came to appreciate the old so I wanted my book cases

to look worn and ancient.

Mike, a magazine art director, one of Mary's terrible "Italians," had become one of my best friends. Mike was fond of cabinetry. He showed me how to make wood look old by wearing it in the right places with the help of things like a wood rasp, nails in gauze and sandpaper.

Gary and Debbie in the rec room of our first house

My "Old" book shelves were successfully given the look of wear and the patina of age. This triumph inspired me to panel the whole recreation room and to turn a corner of it into a small studio.

The absence of a separate studio building and the presence of our young children made late night work mandatory. This was no problem, because I was a late riser. I would do my running around and my research in the remnants of the morning and the afternoon. I devoted the late hours to rendering my illustrations. When I needed models Westport had a number of people who did some part time modeling in addition to professional models. The image of a local postman and part time model probably appeared in more magazines than many movie stars.

Hard at work

Often friends were kind enough to pose and I used Helen a lot. Like everyone else, I worked from photographs, although sometimes I resorted to posing for myself in a mirror. Usually when I posed for myself I made a quick sketch for Helen to follow and had her photograph me. This worked out because I wasn't as fat and ugly as I am today and the photo was only a guide. I turned myself into all kinds of characters.

The fifties and early sixties was a period of quantum change in illustration and advertising. It was an exciting era for a young man amid the excitement of Madison Avenue and Westport.

Coby Whitmore, Jon Whitcomb and Al Parker ruled boy-girl

illustration in female magazines. They were as popular with women as a lot of movie stars.

As the mid point in the century passed a new kind of consumer was waiting in the wings for something new and exciting. A new type of media, television, was on the horizon and projected potent commercial messages into our homes.

Think Small

One day in 1959 I opened a magazine and was blown away when I first saw an ad for a Volkswagen. It was a completely new direction in advertising.

The "think small" ad had been created by a guy named William Bernbach. He was the pied piper who led advertising into a new creative world. His agency, Doyle Dane Bernbach, confined the old ways and old rules to the dust bin of history. The final link in the creative revolution had been forged.

Most experts consider the Volkswagen campaign of the 1960s the best in advertising history. The elongated, exaggerated automobiles set among lush settings with beautiful models were swept away. The little "Beetle," proudly stood unretouched in simple black and white. Truth and simplicity were more powerful arguments than mere fancy. Ads like "Think small" attracted the reader's attention and raised the heights of readership to new levels.

Thanks to William Bernbach, a

generation of clients and creative people began to create ads based on humor, irreverence and often self-deprecation. They had discovered a new and different way to sell products.

Bernbach led the way in having writers and art directors work together like composers and lyricists. Before him writers would originate copy and headlines, which would then be sent to the art department for a visual. The result was too often leaden literalness.

Doyle, Dane and Bernbach went on to produce many more great ads. Their award-winning advertisements were memorable. Among them was the famous "We're number two but we try harder" campaign which positioned Avis against Hertz and the "Plop, plop, fizz, fizz" AlkaSeltzer campaign.

The emergence of D.D.B. cracked open the walls of the great Anglo-Saxon advertising fortresses of Madison Avenue. A new ad generation of advertising arose. Jews, Italians, and even women were breaching the walls on the creative side. In 1967 Mary Wells started Wells, Rich and Greene. She soon rocketed to the top, becoming the highest-paid person in advertising. She was also the first women to head a company listed on

The New York Stock Exchange.

David Ogilvie became the prince charming of Mad Ave. because of the spectacular success of the man with the eye patch ads for Hathaway shirts. His agency, Ogilvie and Mather, was shaking up the deeply entrenched old Titans of Madison Avenue.

The Ogilvie "eye patch man"

Ogilvie's eye patch ads were brilliant. They got noticed because they were daring. To both men and women they denoted action and adventure. More importantly they sold shirts.

David Ogilvie's advertising exploits were the subject of numerous discussions at martini lunches in Madison Avenue bistros and suburban cocktail parties. He had launched his Madison Avenue agency in 1948 with only two people. Within almost no time at all his agency, Ogilvy & Mather, was billing hundreds of millions of dollars worldwide annually.

The "Man with the eye patch" ran exclusively in *The New Yorker*, a "carriage trade" magazine. The campaign was a wild success and became an advertising legend. Hathaway's sales tripled within a couple of years.

With the Hathaway campaign, Ogilvy initiated what came to be called the "Creative Revolution" in advertising. Ad campaigns of originality and power were created when scientific research principals and modern graphic imagery were combined.

Commander Whitehead

Among other things research consisted of luring groups of people into special rooms sometimes equipped with two way mirrors to observe their reaction to various advertising gimmicks. The chairs occupied by the human guinea pigs were often equipped with arms and seat pads that were wired to register reactions.

The mad men observers watched intently, frequently while imbibing their favorite libation in a cigarette engendered fog.

David Ogilvie's great Hathaway campaign was followed by yet another winner. He produced a campaign for Schweppes which featured Commander Whitehead. Whitehead was another wildly effective eccentric. Commander Whitehead's patent line was: "Curiously refreshing." Ogilvy was proclaimed a genius.

In 1957 he rolled out yet another major success. This time it was for Rolls-Royce: "At sixty miles an hour the loudest noise in this new Rolls-Royce comes from the electric clock." A Pierce-Arrow ad in 1933 had made almost exactly the same claim, and with nearly identical wording. Rolls-Royce sales rose fifty percent the following year. Plagiarism didn't seem to bother Ogilvy one whit. He said it was the best ad he had ever written and once again he was an advertising hero.

Ogilvy & Mather prospered mightily. More high profile campaigns followed including one for Puerto Rican tourism, Sears Roebuck, Shell

Oil, and "One-quarter cleansing cream," Dove soap.

The great advertising legend died in 1999 in his sprawling 14th-century French castle.

One of the most popular of the early television campaigns was a series of TV commercials staring Burt and Harry Peal for Peals Beer. Burt and Harry were very funny and so entertaining that the public's attention was totally on them. The public was so enraptured with their witticisms that it didn't notice what they were selling. They made the TV audience happy, but alas not the sponsor, Peal's Beer went down the drain.

One of my friends was the senior vice president of an agency that had a major headache medicine as a client. The TV ads they put on for their client were some of the most disliked ads of all time. They consisted mostly of a hammer pounding inside a grimacing guy's head with a voice over.

I asked my buddy why he put such god awful ads on the tube? He responded that the medicine was flying off the shelves. He said that the ads were so irritating that people remembered the name!

My favorite advertising coups occurred before I got to Madison Avenue. As the story goes, in 1942 The American Tobacco Company decided that Lucky Strike cigarettes needed a new package. In the early days of WWII patriotic fervor was at a fever pitch. People were even donating their precious aluminum pots and pans to the war effort.

The American Tobacco Company offered the world famous industrial designer, Raymond Lowey, fifty thousand dollars to design a new package. He had created the logos for Esso, Shell, AT&T and Coca-Cola.

Fifty thousand clams went a long way when just the year before $650 would purchase a new full sized Ford or Chevy. In 1942 you couldn't buy a new car for any price.

Lowey accepted. He brought back their same design with only one change. He dropped the green background behind the red circle. The client was left with a package sporting a red circle on a pristine white background. They were also left with a bill for fifty grand.

Lest we feel sorry for The American Tobacco Company they saved more than fifty thousand dollars in a jiffy with their savings on green ink.

A pre war Lucky Strike package

Introducing a new package for a major brand is no small matter. This hot potato was handed to their ad agency, Lord & Thomas, a Chicago advertising agency. The agency came up with one of the most brilliant slogans in advertising history, "Lucky Strike Green Has Gone To War!"

Cigarette smokers stampeded into the stores to buy the patriotic coffin nails that had sacrificed so much for the war effort!

Helena Rubinstein, one of the first people to make a great fortune in cosmetics, was asked the secret of her success. She replied that it was "The knowledge that women will not buy a cosmetic that costs less than a dollar!" It must be noted that this utterance was made during the time when people made a great deal of their purchases in five and dime stores. It should be further noted that one of their biggest cosmetic purchases was cold cream. Cold cream was, and perhaps still is, nothing more than refined pig fat.

Charles Revson, a great cosmetic mogul of the post war period was very sadistic. He loved to call meetings with key people from his company's agency around dinner time, just after working hours. He would then, during the meeting, enjoy a cocktail and a savory dinner without offering anything to the agency people. He controlled one of the biggest and most lucrative advertising accounts, otherwise no big agency would have touched his company. Some still wouldn't.

Advertising can be a wise investment producing great wealth. It can also be a place to pour money down a rat hole as fast as gambling with your eyes closed.

My exaggerated definition of advertising was "Ten percent ability and ninety percent bull shit." Today, with all the scientific principals employed in producing ads my old definition would have to be altered. However a lot of the latter percentage would remain.

A slogan of only a few words and a few pictures can create the desire for a product that can make millions for an advertiser. A good example might be the four simple words that were combined each time a handsome worker or a pretty girl was shown drinking a Coca-Cola. They propelled Coca-Cola's sales into the stratosphere. The four words were: "The pause that refreshes."

The idea of taking a break on a long trip or during a day's work and relaxing with a refreshing drink was planted in millions of heads. And the drink that was planted in peoples' heads was Coke.

The average person can only read seven words on a billboard at highway speeds so the shorter the slogan the better.

The artist chosen to illustrate the ads was Hadden Sunbloom. He was terrific at portraying wholesome, healthy looking guys and gals. He was perfect for the job but the demand for his work was so great that a number of illustrators began aping his style of painting. They were known as members of the "Sunbloom School of Illustration."

Madison Avenue was a synonym for advertising but not all

A mid-century *Coke* ad

agencies were actually located on Madison Avenue. I did a lot of work for a large agency located on Wall Street. Their clients were mostly big financial firms and institutions such as banks and insurance companies.

Whenever I had to pick up or deliver a job from that agency, I avoided the heavy traffic in Manhattan by tooling down East River Drive in whatever sports car I had at the time, heading straight to Wall Street. I would then park right in front of the agency building ignoring the no parking sign. The fine for parking was fifteen dollars and I got a ticket about every third time. It cost around five dollars to park in a parking garage a few blocks away. I just sent in the fine money and enjoyed the convenience. Other people must have caught on to this sweet deal because after a few years the fine was raised to fifty dollars.

I was invited to a big agency Christmas party at a club on the west side of town. It was near the Museum of Modern Art and I miraculously found a parking place by the museum.

Booze flowed like Niagara and the witty conversation of creative people combined with all the pretty girls made it hard to leave. But leave I must because I had to join Helen at her brother's apartment on the East River for a late dinner.

My memory of that night is fogged to my prodigious consumption of alcohol. I remember that my marriage vows were challenged by an invitation from two pretty girls to accompany them to their digs down in Greenwich Village for some sexual exercise.

It was a struggle but I bid the attractive young ladies adieu and went to find my car. I couldn't find it. I searched everywhere around the museum but no car.

I have, as through-a-glass-darkly, memories of walking the streets looking for the car. I also had a dim memory of hiring a cab and riding around looking for it along with an even dimmer memory of the inside of a bar and reporting the car stolen at a police station.

When my head began to clear I was leaning against a lamppost like the typical cartoon. It was bright daylight and I was way over on the

East Side of Manhattan very near Helen's brother's building.

To say that Helen was mad as hell would be an understatement but as always Helen could not stay mad for long.

Several days later we received a call from Helen's brother, John. He had found our car! It was parallel parked only a few doors from his building and was festooned with parking tickets. Fortunately I had reported the car stolen so the tickets were forgiven.

The realization, that I had driven the car in heavy traffic across the most densely packed part of Manhattan in a drunken stupor, caused me to break out into a cold sweat. The fact that I had parked the car perfectly in a narrow slot amazed me. I don't think I could have done it as well cold sober.

Ad or "mad men" spoke a very colorful language. They worked on Mad Ave or "The avenue" and often referred to themselves as hucksters but didn't like to be called that by outsiders. Some restaurateurs opened a new restaurant on Madison Avenue which they named "Hucksters." Mad men spent a lot of time in restaurants and bars shelling out money on booze and cigarettes. The name was a big mistake because the advertising people were outraged. The name was quickly changed.

I loved the witty phrases of ad speak. Phrases like, "Let's run it up the flagpole and see if anyone salutes," or "Let's put it on the train and see if it gets off in Westport," abounded.

Many great ad campaigns were born on napkins in restaurants and bars amid martinis and clouds of cigarette smoke. People in the trade worked hard, but played even harder.

Advertising was a "Take no prisoners business" for an illustrator. The money was very good but you had to meet deadlines and come up with something good every time, no matter what. Whenever I delivered a tough assignment and the art director liked it, the pressure was off. Then it was party time in spades. If there was a party going on in town, which was often the case, I enjoyed it like a cowboy coming into town after a long hard cattle drive.

More than a few suburbanite illustrators of my acquaintance maintained private studios in the city. They were used for more than business. Mid century people were just as promiscuous as they are today. However, they were less open about their activities.

Advertising has become a multibillion dollar industry. Without the demand for products that it engenders our great free enterprise system could not function.

As the second decade after the war dawned improved photography slowly began to push illustration out of advertising. However, television had not yet destroyed the short story magazines that fed many illustrators as well as writers.

One illustration that stands out in my memory, was an illustration depicting a man coming ashore from a shipwreck. Wet clothes cling to people in particular ways and I knew that this would require a wet model. It was winter in New England. Even indoors I would find it difficult to ask someone to pose in wet clothes. I had to grin and bear it myself.

The shipwreck victim needed to be in an old life jacket so I set out in the old prewar Austin sedan that I owned to procure one. I had bought a lot of stuff for costumes from a local army and navy store. The owner told me he would be happy to loan me a very old life jacket that was in his possession.

It was very cold but the roads appeared to be clear of ice and snow. I came around a corner and suddenly encountered a solid sheet of ice. The little Austin rolled over and over and came to rest on one side. I tumbled around inside (this was before the advent of seat belts) and I vividly remember that all I was thinking about was being concerned that the old borrowed life jacket might get dirty!

Despite the tumble I wasn't hurt and since the little vehicle was on its side the door was on top. I had to chin myself to rise out of the car. Two men stopped their truck and with their help the Austin was turned right side up. Miraculously the only damage to the old Austin was a small dent in one side and the loss of the door handles. They had been shorn off on one side. They must have made the old cars out of heavier steel than today because that little sedan was like a tank.

I thanked the guys that helped me. Then I got into the car on the side that had doors that would open and drove home. I drove the Austin around like that for months afterward. The only inconvenience being that I had to get in on the passenger side and slide over onto the driver's side. It would have cost more than the car was worth to fix it. There was also some kind of perverse pleasure in driving a car that kept going despite its body wounds.

Our little Austin

When I arrived back home with the borrowed life jacket, which had come through the accident unscathed, I gave Helen a rough sketch of the photo I wanted. Next I set up the lights and the camera just outside a bathroom door. When I emerged staggering like a survivor from the shower fully clothed and wearing the life jacket she took several pictures. I then quickly got into some dry clothes.

I put myself staggering onto the beach, barefooted with wet, clinging clothes, into the foreground of the illustration. In the background I created a raging storm with an angry surf and a stricken, sinking ship in the distance. I remember that the art director liked the job, so it was all worth the effort.

Figure height in illustrations was exaggerated according to the type of illustration

Many wasted hours have been spent arguing over whether illustration is art. One thing is certain, an illustration is usually not the same thing as a pretty picture. The painting of a bowl of flowers done from life can be a beautiful work of fine art but it depicts something that exists. Most often an illustration depicts something imagined or something that once existed. An illustration frequently requires research. For instance if a scene of Columbus landing in the new world is to be created, the illustrator must know what he and his men wore and such details as the fact that the flag of Castile, not Spain, was carried.

Men, especially heroic types, in illustrations are taller than in real life, usually eight heads tall except for fashion illustration, they are nine heads tall. Women, especially heroines, are almost always beautiful. The poses are dramatic, in fact things are exaggerated just like in the old silent movies.

Models for my illustrations were found in my family, and in my many friends who kindly agreed to pose for me along with the cadre of local professional and local part time models.

Friends posing for illustrations

Here are a few of the different illustration techniques I employed. I was always trying new ways to do things. This is not a good idea because it prevents one from becoming really good at one thing. All the really top illustrators that I knew usually worked in a single technique that they were masters of.

    I never mastered anything because I was always trying different techniques.

My forte was line drawing which is just pure draftmanship. In the past when reproduction technology was not as advanced as today line art was very popular. It was easy to reproduce but very unforgiving of mistakes by the artist.
The illusion of three dimensional form within a simple line drawing could be conveyed by the artist but it was not easy. The appearance of light and shadow could also be conveyed by "painting in line."

Today line illustration is little used because of the simplicity of reproduction. The art of simple drawing is passing away.

CONFESSIONS OF A MADMAN 100

101 CONFESSIONS OF A MADMAN

Teeming Talent

Westport was somewhat unique among small towns in having a sizable number of professional models among its citizenry. One, an extremely beautiful girl who was one of New York's top models taught a Sunday school class at the Greene's Farms Congregational Church. Helen also taught a Sunday school class there.

The beautiful young model seemed to be happily married to a young New York attorney. I had met him in the bar car on the train from New York and he seemed like a perfectly normal guy.

One day the television screen exploded with the news that a bomb had blown up an airliner over Bolivia, North Carolina. The name of the town, Bolivia, stuck in my mind because of the unusual name.

The news of a bomb blowing up an airplane was nothing compared to the thunderbolt that struck me next. The suicide bomber was the husband of Helen's beautiful, fellow Sunday school teacher!
The "forty-four and ninty-nine percent pure" Ivory Soap girl burst forth as the star of a much hyped hard core porn movie titled, *Behind the Green Door*. Needless to say Ivory Soap hurriedly removed her from the soap box.

Debra, our daughter was and still is a great beauty and was in demand as a model by local artists. One of my close friends asked me "How does such an ugly bastard have such a beautiful daughter?" To this I replied "We must have had a handsome delivery man."

Ward Brackett, another friend, and one of the nation's best illustrators, requested Debra to pose for a portrait. It was the main focus of his book on painting as well as for the cover. He kindly offered to give us the painting which was worth many thousands of dollars. Beautiful women abounded on the covers that Ward painted for America's

Debbie is the little girl pining the flower on her mother In this magazine cover. I used Helen for the two ladies in the back and myself for both the men.

top woman's magazines but he had something special to say about Debra in his book. "Debbie made a very pretty subject. She has a flawless complexion, good coloring and regular features. In fact, she is so attractive

I could see that it might be difficult to keep the portrait from looking like a soap ad."

When one of my closest friends, Ed Vebell was selected to design

This is a portrait of our daughter, Debbie, painted by an old friend Ward Brackett for his popular book on portrait painting

and illustrate a United States postage stamp saluting "American Youth," he chose Debra to represent American youth along with three other kids.

Most of our friends in Westport tended to be illustrators or art directors but several of our closest friends were industrial designers and one was a television news anchor. Harry Reasoner became one of the nation's top TV news personalities and at Harry and his wife Kay's parties, we met many other famous people in the world of television.

The Westport Artists had a dinner and a show focusing on one of the members works each month. These monthly dinners were a great place to meet, swap stories and become inspired by seeing the work of some the best in the business. In addition to the regular monthly dinners there were frequent parties to which wives and girlfriends were invited.

It was interesting to observe that the members who did their work at home and only went into New York when necessary came to the dinners well dressed and that the members who commuted into the city regularly came to the dinners very casually dressed. I suppose that those of us who went around all week casually dressed looked for an excuse to

Debbie is the girl on the left in this U.S. postage stamp illustrated by my good friend Edward Vebell

get dressed up and the others felt just the opposite.

One monthly dinner and show stands out in my mind because of a response given by Robert Fawcette, the featured member. Bob Fawcette could portray the interiors of Gothic mansions and period English scenes like no other. His color had a warm antique feeling to it that was almost magical. His illustrations for a series of Sherlock Holmes stories for *Colliers Magazine* were so wonderful that they made one feel that he had been born just to illustrate Sherlock Holmes.

Bob mentioned in his talk about the exhibition of his work that he was color blind. This provoked the question from one of his fellow members as to how his work had such great color.

Robert Fawcette's answer will always live in my memory. He replied "Oh hell I just read the names on the tubes!"

During my early years I had a New York art representative named Clinton Shepherd. Shep was a much older man than I, but so were most of my other friends and colleagues. It is a mystery to me as to why he acted as an art rep because he was a very talented artist himself. A large bronze monument of a World War I soldier which sits in the middle of the Boston Post Road in Westport was sculpted by him.

Shep felt that I should become a member of the New York Society of Illustrators. Samples of my work were submitted to the proper committee and to my delight I was deemed worthy of membership.

The society owns and occupies a prestigious building on East Sixty Third Street between Lexington and Park Avenues. It became the place where I often had lunch when I was in the city. It was a great place to take clients to lunch and to transact business with clients and people like Shep.

The National Cartoonist Society did not have a building of their own. Our club made our facilities open to them as a brother organization.

Many of the most famous cartoonists were frequently there. Rube Goldberg, who will always live in the dictionary for his outlandish cartoon machinery, had lunch there most every day. He always sat at a big round table for the members who were there by themselves. If I didn't have a luncheon guest I also sat at that table and got to converse with many famous people.

The society had a number of evening events throughout the year to which wives and girlfriends were invited. Once a year it put on a theatrical show called *Artists and Models*. The club was awash in theatrical talent and gag writers. Unlike me, I have discovered over the years that many illustrators and cartoonists are multitalented. For instance, Otto Soglow the creator of *The Little King*, one of the top comic strips of the past, was one of the best comic magicians I have ever seen.

All the talent put into the effort, plus the beautiful scantily-clothed models, and the fact that Broadway in those days could not be so risqué, created a real hoot. The show was put on for two nights. Black tie was required for the second night and when he could make it, Bob Hope flew in from the coast to see it.

I was told that *Artists and Models* was made into a Broadway show long before my time and that the royalties from it paid for the Societies' building.

New York City is about forty-five miles from Westport and it took about an hour by train. When I had to go into "town" I most often took the train that left a little after ten in the morning. That train seemed to be the one that soap opera actors and other TV people used. I guess that got them into town in time for makeup and rehearsals. Theater, TV and movie people had their own circle just as we illustrators and artists had ours.

Westport and its environs, when I lived there, was the home of Bette Davis, Boris Karloff, Leonard Bernstein and many other famous people. The only famous movie star in Westport that I knew was Paul

Newman's wife, Joanne Woodward but she was not on speaking terms with me. The only major TV personality that I knew fairly well was Harry Reasoner and his wife Kay. We had been neighbors.

There was a bar car on one of the late afternoon trains from NY. I tried to make it whenever I could because it was a rolling cocktail party. Usually I had so much fun it was a disappointment when I reached my destination. Often the contents of this mobile party spilled out of the merry capsule into Marrio's. Marrio's was a restaurant and bar which had the good fortune to be located just across the narrow street from the little Saugatuck Railroad station in Westport. Marrio must have been a happy man because his bar had eager customers fighting to get up to his bar and thrust cash into his paws.

It is a wonder that those of us from those heady days of the past survived. It seems that the consumption of alcohol was truly oceanic. It was not unusual for the ad people I frequently entertained at lunch to consume two or three martinis at lunch and then go back to work. Many executives had bars in their offices and drinks were often consumed during meetings.

The people who fell out of the bar car would have to drive home. And some of them had a long drive. Most people drank hard liquor at parties, not wine and beer as today. I have to confess that I too consumed too much booze, but I never could drink a martini. One martini would have put me off my feet. If I drank too much it became just like a quick-acting sleeping pill.

Helen and I had a lot of parties and it was not too unusual for some of our guests to still be there when the sun came up. We worked hard and played hard.

All this booze was consumed amid clouds of smoke. People smoked from the time they got up in the morning until they went to bed. Ashtrays were on every table and desk and in every vehicle in the land.

The door opener to a job in a prestigious ad agency was a degree from an Ivy League university. Of course many other people were able to get a foot in the door. For instance a recommendation from a client was a major hasp lifter.

However, once in the door the first step on the ladder was the mail room. It was said that the best dressed men (women were as rare as whale's teeth, except as secretaries and stenos) in the agency were found in the mail room.

Often, those in publishing, as well as those starting at the bottom in advertising, were paid so little that wealthy parents were needed to subsidize the new recruits. This had been the case with Helen when she had started working for Crowell Collier Publishing Company.

She had worked herself up to a copy writing job which she left when we were married. Most women in those days chose to be homemakers rather than work at a profession.

Puddle Jump

Soon after we were married Helen and I took our first of trip overseas. Helen had been to Europe while she was still going to Mount Holyoke and she loved to travel. She spoke fluent French with a beautiful Parisian accent and some Spanish which was of immense help when we traveled.

Pan American Airlines advertised a special three week round-trip airfare to Europe for $325. The feature, other than the price was that you could enter the continent in Lisbon and exit in London. You could stop off as much as you wanted as long as you went on a more or less continuous route. You could also do the trip in reverse, London to Lisbon if you chose. We chose Lisbon to London.

Helen arranged everything. We landed in Lisbon but we stayed in a seaside hotel in Cascais a resort only a short trolly ride outside Lisbon. From there we hired a car and driver and saw all the main sites in that part of Portugal on both sides of the Tagus River. Helen did her homework

Helen with our car and driver in Portugal

before every trip we took, nothing was missed. The driver we hired in Cascais spoke English with an upper class accent. He could have passed himself off as an English earl. But he had never been to England. It seems that Cascais was a favorite watering hole for Brit nobility. He had learned his English from the peerage.

From Lisbon we flew to Seville, it was not on our direct route. We had to use another airline at extra cost but it was worth it. Helen had arranged a car rental. We saw the sites in Seville and drove around the Andalusian region of Spain visiting Granada and Malaga and ending up in Alicante. While we were in Granada we visited the Alhambra. We enjoyed the beautiful Alhambra so much that we visited it on all four of our trips back to Spain.

Just before we ended up in Algiciras we spent a couple of days in a delightful little seaside town called Marbella. We didn't know before we got there that it had just been discovered by the Duke and Duchess of Windsor, the arbiters of the jet set. Wherever the king, who gave up his throne for love went the hoi polloi were sure to follow. The owners of our new luxury hotel there had not yet received the word that they were now the "in" spot. Our spacious quarters cost us only four bucks a night.

We surrendered our little rental car on the dock at Aligiciras and boarded a boat for Tangier in Morocco. I was concerned about how we would find our way around once we got there as we didn't speak Arabic. It wasn't an Indo-European language so there were no root words to give us any clues, as we pulled in to the dock all I could see was a sea of Arabs and Berbers, my concern was intensified.

Much to my pleasant surprise when we stepped off the gangplank onto the continent of Africa a tall man with a red fez on his head greeted us by name. He was attired in the garb of a Berber but with some difference. A stripped regimental tie and an oxford shirt with a button down collar showed under his jellaba, the traditional robe worn by Berbers. His was

Helen the great camel jockey

Resplendent in my woolen grey flannel "Madison Avenue uniform" in the fierce Moroccan heat

not traditional, it was made of gray flannel not the usual stripped type.

As he called out our names and greeted us he bowed using the hand gestures of North Africa. He introduced himself and stated that he was our guide and was at our service. He had a taxi waiting and within a few minutes we were ushered into the exotic Al Menza Hotel. Helen had once again taken care of everything!

During the next several days we toured Tangier, visited the Casaba, enjoyed some exotic nightlife, did a little shopping and rode camels around the countryside of Morocco.

The next phase of the whirlwind adventure, managed by my lovely wife, consisted of a flight from Tangier to Madrid. This put us back on the route covered by our original airfare.

We visited all the main sites, and wined and dined in Ernest Hemmingway's favorite haunts. Then we topped off our evenings sipping excellent Spanish cognac under the stars in Madrid's great Plaza Major.

Helen in Madrid

Before continuing our journey by air Helen's desire to wine and dine in another of Hemmingway's hangouts required us to take a side trip to Segovia. There we supped in an old restaurant near the famous Roman aqueduct where the famous novelist had dinned on roast suckling pig. We also dinned on the wee pigs.

When years later we revisited that same restaurant with our children in tow. We once again dined on roast suckling pig. However, this time any appetite I'd had for roast suckling pig was destroyed. I looked down at my plate and saw a tiny ear attached to my portion of miniature pork. I could not eat it. When we left and were outside the restaurant and I heard the faint squeal of a baby pig. My revulsion was reinforced.

The next day we were off to Paris. Helen knew her way around Paris like a native. She had spent time there while she was in college. She could easily pass as an upper crust French lady because of her French accent. We were treated with deference by the French. People deemed to be upper crust are deferenced almost everywhere for no good reason.

This was my first visit to Paris and it occurred not too long after the war. I was excited to see all the buildings pock marked by machine-gun bullets near a bridge that led over to the Ile de Cite. I had remembered seeing film of the fighting around this very spot, it was taken as Paris fell to the Allies. Paris was as beautiful as it was reputed to be. People seemed to spend a huge amount of their time outside in sidewalk cafes. When I commented on this, someone remarked that it was because the average building was over a hundred years old and it was not so great inside.

Our only disappointment was the fact that we were denied entrance into Maximes Restaurant. I was not in a tuxedo even though I had on a jacket and tie. Helen was very frugal about most things but she had never met a meal or a bottle of wine that was too expensive. Frankly, I was relieved that we were denied admittance. To me, today's gourmet meal is tomorrow's garbage. Needless to say I was never foolish enough to say

An illustration of the London blitz

that to my wife.

After Paris we were off to see the sites of London. Paris had few scars of the war but not so London. There were still areas where only the ruble from the blitz had been cleaned up. Since rebuilding activity had been going on for several years the old city must have been hit hard. As with the other cities we had visited Helen saw to it that we saw everything of importance. Since Hemingway was not a big habitué of London this time it was Charles Dickens and Samuel Johnson who were the focus. Their dining and wining haunts had to be frequented by us.

Because confession is good for the soul, let me admit here, my formal education having been sorely neglected, that I didn't know of Samuel Johnson's importance to our language, because he was the father of the English dictionary.

In all the cities we visited I was in total agreement with all the places we spent our time. The one exception was the time spent in the great museums. I had to press to spend more time in the Prado, the Louvre and the British Museum. Helen saw to it that no time was wasted. We were always on the go, we even saw places most people rarely see like, El Grecco's house in Spain.

When we flew home I was exhausted. She had exposed the hick

from the hills of Tennessee to a whirlwind tour of history, art, architecture, and literature.

Not too long after returning I became involved in a sideline business with a close cartoonist friend. Lloyd had a successful national syndicated strip which provided him with a good income but like most of us, he was interested in more. This was the period when "Paint by the number pictures" were the rage. One of us had the idea that "Paint by the numbers greeting cards" would also be popular. We proceeded to put together a boxed kit containing a set of greeting cards. They were accompanied by water colors and brushes with a full color guide sheet. All one had to do to produce a custom hand colored greeting card was to paint inside the lines on the cards following the guide sheet.

We engaged a salesman who, for a commission, showed the dummy product to some buyers. It was enthusiastically received, and armed with good reports from buyers, we proceeded to order 50,000 set up boxes. They had full color wrappers and all the other ingredients necessary for 50,000 kits. We found a company in nearby Bridgeport, Connecticut that specialized in assembling and sending out direct mail items. A price per kit for storage and assembly was negotiated, hands were shaken and we were in business.

Orders came in from such diverse places as Saks Fifth Avenue and F.W. Woolworth. The stores were excited about the new item, but alas the store customers were not. Our "Paint by the numbers greeting cards" gathered dust on the store shelves. Saks Fifth Avenue and F.W. Woolworth didn't get rich having their stock gather dust. They clamored to cancel orders and to try to return the unsold kits.

Lloyd and I had a first class mess on our hands. The sweet little sideline business that was going to produce some easy money for us with little work on our part had turned into a complete disaster.

To make matters worse the owner of the company in Bridgeport, rumored to have ties to the Mafia, was reneging on our agreement. He demanded an outrageous sum to release our material.

A company was located that would buy all of our unsold kits for a portion of the wholesale price. We would not make any money but we wouldn't take a bath.

We had become friends with the salesman for the big printing company in New Haven, Connecticut that had printed the boxes. He persuaded his company to send down a truck to Bridgeport to pick up our stuff. They would put the kits together for the original price that had been agreed on by the Bridgeport company.

The cavalry was coming over the hill to our rescue with bugles blowing. But a big wall stood in their path. Tony the Bridgeport guy was demanding blood money to ransom our stuff.

An idea struck me like a skyrocket on the fourth of July. Why not con Tony into releasing our goods? I had never had any experience with nefarious things of that sort, but I had read that dishonest people are the easiest people to fool. Tony qualified in that department.

I knew that I had to excite his greed and that it had to be done in such a way as to seem like something most people wouldn't touch.

The current news provided just the thing! The Dominican Republic was ruled by a ruthless dictator named Rafael Trujillo. He had been in the news for the terrible way he had treated his people. The American public had only recently been appalled to learn that Franklin Roosevelt Jr., the son of their beloved wartime president, had accepted a job to handle public relations for Trujillo.

I had shown Tony some of the company magazines that Stringfellow, Pope and Morimoto did for major international corporations. I remembered that he had been impressed. The setup was perfect. I played it like a well-tuned violin.

My approach to Tony was friendly but a little cagey, as if I was being cautious in approaching him with a shady deal. I told him that Stringfellow, Pope and Morimoto had been asked by Franklin Roosevelt's PR firm to produce a monthly magazine. It would extol the virtues of Gen. Trujillo. I told him that most people wouldn't touch it because of the stigma. Because of that we were told that money was no object. The money was so terrific we couldn't turn it down. The only problem was distribution. He was the only person I knew who could handle that part of the job. If he was in on the deal, he could almost name his own price for his services.

He took the hook. While he was salivating on thoughts of all the money he was going to make, I produced a check for the sum we legitimately owed. I then had him sign a paper releasing all our goods, I acted as if it was an afterthought.

The next day, while greedy thoughts of shady profit were still dancing in Tony's head, a truck showed up and our property was liberated.

For years afterwards whenever my friend Lloyd and I got together we had a good laugh when one of us wondered if Tony was still waiting on the magazines he was to distribute.

For a long time I had dreamed of living on a tropical island, and at the tender age of twenty-six, I convinced Helen that we should give it a try. The art director of *Red Book magazine* had a house on a hill overlooking the harbor at Charlotte Amelia on Saint Thomas in the Virgin Islands. He agreed to rent us his house. He cautioned us to look out for the little poison tablets in the closets. He knew that we had two small children. The tablets were to kill the bugs common to the tropics.

I was very fond of Helen's mother so I was happy to have her come along. The five of us were soon on our way via San Juan in Puerto Rico. The minute our taxi stopped in front of the house we had rented both kids burst out of the car as if they had been shot out of a canon. They were in the house almost before we could get out.

Thinking of the poison tablets, I rushed into the house to remove them. To my horror my daughter Debra announced that her little brother Gary had found some candy on the floor in a closet. Fortunately, the taxi had not left as luggage was still being unloaded. I screamed for Helen to hold the taxi. I stuck my finger down little Gary's throat trying to get him to throw up. That didn't work. I had the taxi take him along with the rest of us to the island hospital as fast as the taxi would go. They had to pump his stomach quickly or he would die. The only stomach pump the hospital had was for adults. There was no choice, they had to force it down the nose of a little two year old. Gary's screams of pain were hard to endure, but his life was saved.

Little Gary

After that our days on Saint Thomas were pure bliss. It was 1956 and the island was largely undiscovered by the mass tourist trade. We frequently went swimming on the beach at Megan's Bay, one of the most beautiful beaches in the Caribbean and we were most often the only people there.

There was an old building with extremely thick stone walls down by the waterfront in Charlotte Amelia. It housed a restaurant called Higgins' Gate. We spent many happy hours there drinking rum and dancing the Meringue to the steel band. The music reverberated off the thick walls. We often spent the cocktail hour on our terrace and watched the tropical sunset through the palms. In the evening the view of the harbor with all the lights and all the ships was spectacular.

A calypso singer called King Sparrow was a legend throughout the Caribbean. He was a master of true calypso where the words are made up as the song is sung. Helen and I both were fortunate to be sitting in the first row one night in a restaurant when the great Calypso singer was performing. He came over and sang a verse about each of us. I was honored that we had been the subject of a verse by the great "Sparrow."

There were only two hotels on Saint Thomas of any size and one small hotel with only fifteen rooms. The small hotel was situated up on the mountain overlooking Charlotte Amelia and it was for sale for twenty-five thousand dollars. If we sold our house in Westport we could raise that sum.

Even though we were living in a tropical paradise, we didn't fit in. Although everyone was friendly, both black and white and we were frequently entertained and invited to parties by the Continentals (Caucasian residents) who were mostly rich and retired. The few young people were mostly hippie types.

My career in illustration would have had to be given up because we were just too far from everything. Illustration was what I was born to do. I am glad we had a taste of what it would be like to give up the rat race because we now had it out of our system. We were glad to get back to Westport and to plunge into the race with newfound vigor.

I was able to quickly get back into gear. Most of my sources of work had not dried up as I had feared. Soon I was again busy at the profession that I loved.

It is my belief that earning a living doing something that is enjoyable is far more important than making a lot of money doing something that's not enjoyable. Perhaps carpenters enjoy their work more than people who shuffle papers all day.

Dream House

Helen, the kids and I were very happy in our comfortable split level on Guyer Road. It was on the top of a hill and had a nice view from the back over a little undeveloped valley, it was also near the beaches on Long Island Sound. The only problem was that it was in a development. Everyone had a half acre and all the houses resembled each other.

My dream was to have a house that was completely unusual, and one day I found it!

The instructions that we had given to the real estate agent we had engaged were very specific. We were only to be called if a house, that was old, completely different and unusual, came on the market. It also had to be somewhere near our price range. I told her that there was no hurry because we were very happy where we were.

Many months went by before she called. Then she told me that the house I was looking for had just been listed. I dropped what I was working on and sped to the site. The house was exactly what we had dreamed about. I called Helen to come immediately. Within fifteen minutes we had handed the real estate broker a check to seal the deal.

It was fortunate that we had acted as quickly as we did because the spouse of another purchaser, a sculptor, was enroute from New York to buy the house.

Dream houses may vary as much as faces. This is fortunate because if our houses looked as much alike as our automobiles and our refrigerators, this would be a boring world.

Our dream house certainly fulfilled its role in making the world less boring. To begin with it was a copy of a fourteenth century Norman house in Cornwall, on the English coast. It set up on a hill overlooking Valley Road in Westport not far from the beach. The property that went with the house consisted of four lots. It was so heavily forested that in the summer no other houses could be seen from it. On one side there was a cliff and the house was approached by a long winding driveway.

Inside the house all the rooms had fireplaces, beamed ceilings and beautiful old wide planked floors. Some of the floors were carpeted. The walls were either paneled or plastered to look like the chalk of the house copied in Cornwall.

The copy was not exact of course because our new house had modern plumbing and central heating. The roof, while properly steep, was not thatched as the other house. It was also much larger having been added to by the previous owners who had kept the original architecture. I was told that the house had been owned by a well known pianist.

Harold Ward, the man who had built the house back in the 1930s lived nearby in what had once been his guest house. Harold had been one of the first pilots in the Royal Flying Corps, the forerunner of the Royal Air Force. He had the British Empire flying license number eight and was one of only a small handful of military pilots in the world in August, 1914 when the first world war erupted.

Harold's father had been in the Parliament during that war and was a friend of Winston Churchill's. Churchill at that time was the First Lord of the Admiralty. Harold had helped train pilots in the Italian Air Force during that war. He was called back to England and invited to breakfast with Churchill.

Churchill asked Harold to appear to vanish and secretly go to Russia. The October revolution had taken Russia out of the war and a civil war was raging. Anti Bolshevik forces led by General Yudenich were in one part uf the country and forces led by Admiral Kolchack and General Denikin were in other parts of the country trying to prevent a communist takeover.

England was secretly trying to help the anti-Bolshevicks set up an airforce. Harold's mission was to organize training for the pilots. Airplanes

A Russian revolution illustration

were planned to be covertly supplied to General Yudenich. Alas pilots were trained but no planes were ever shipped. The British government had changed its mind. They did send a destroyer which rescued Harold and a few others. General Yudenich and his men probably met a grim fate.

One of my most serious regrets is that I didn't get a tape recorder and spend a few hours recording Harold telling me about his time with General Yudenich. All this is lost to history. Everybody involved fighting the Reds was no doubt shot or died in the Gulags. Their writings were erased. I had asked Harold to get a tape recorder and relate his adventures, but he never did.

The living room in our new house was reasonably spacious with a nice fireplace and beamed ceilings but it wasn't unusual enough for me. I decided that what the house needed was a three level living room. The three levels should possess an old English bar tucked away in a big nook, a huge fireplace and a big conversation pit. The other requirement was that it needed to look like it was built five hundred years ago but with modern features.

Money for this project presented a problem. The problem was mitigated by my hiring a young man named Grover Mills. He had worked as a model and done odd jobs for me. He lived at home, so he only needed modest pay. Grover was eager for a job during his summer break from the University of Bridgeport. He had spent a couple of years in South America in the Peace Corps and was a very resourceful young man. He was not an experienced builder. I couldn't afford an experienced builder so Grover had to fit the bill.

The fact that the house was secluded, away from the eyes of building inspectors and building trade unions, was a big help to my modest building fund.

Grover appeared one warm June day and announced that he was free for the summer and eager to get to work. I told him that the project had to be completed during his summer break. This mandated an immediate building start.

He looked a little shaken when he was informed that there were no plans. There were only some quick scribbles done on an old sheet of paper as we talked. I told him that it should be built like they built houses in the fifteenth century, with only rudimentary plans. That was my approach to ending up with something that looked five centuries old.

One of the existing bedrooms was to be used as the uppermost level of the new living room. The old living room would become the big new master bedroom. I had procured a truly massive sledge hammer from somewhere, and I said something like "Oh hell, here we go." Then I took a mighty swing at the masonry pseudo-chalk wall in the bedroom that had to be removed. I then handed the big hammer to Grover and told him to have at it. Dust and pieces of cement were flying in every direction. Helen came in and greeted the scene with a look of horror. In my eagerness to get the job underway nothing in the bedroom had been removed.

Helen was too busy frantically getting her stuff out of the way to turn her wrath on me. Fortunately, the ceiling didn't fall down and most of the summer was spent with only plastic sheeting separating the indoors from the elements.

A major impediment was encountered when a rock as big as washing machine was uncovered. It stood in Grover's way. The rock was unusual in that its grain went in every direction. It defied blows from my big sledge hammer. It was too big to move and it could not be dynamited as it was too close to the house. Grover tried heating it with a blow torch that was almost a flame thrower. Then it was dowsed with ice water while still hot, but nothing fazed it.

A jackhammer contractor was called in. When asked what his hourly rate was he informed me that he didn't work by the hour. He only worked by contract and produced one. I had hoped to save some money by having it done on an hourly rate but I had no choice. The papers were signed and he got to work. He spent untold hours of ear splitting work and spent a small fortune replacing drill bits before the giant rock finally became a big pile of normal sized rocks.

The contractor told me that he rued his refusal to take on the job on an hourly basis. He had lost his shirt. He said that my rock was the toughest rock he had run into in all his years in business.

The big, bad boulder had morphed into some of the best looking rocks that Grover and I had ever seen. They were put to good use in the big fireplace and for the wall in the conversation pit. The fireplace was large enough for a very large cast iron pot to be swung over the fire for cooking as in days of yore.

About that time a treasure trove of wonderful things to

incorporate in my new room was discovered. I found a place in a nearby town that sold recovered junk from a wrecking company. It abounded with old windows, paneling, wooden beams, ancient wrought iron gates and a myriad of other treasures. They had been salvaged from old buildings that were torn down. At the time I bought everything I needed as the prices were very low. Later on the prices for salvaged treasures went up like a rocket.

Thanks to my bargain purchases my new room had beautiful old chestnut beams and very tall narrow casement windows. An old ornate wrought iron gate became a glass window and was built into one of the walls next to the fireplace. Salvaged carved oak paneling from an old mansion and a copper counter top gave my old English bar the proper look. A collection of antique ale tankards were the cherry on the icing.

A big antique oak dinning table lowered to cocktail table height filled the space between the red velvet seats in the cocktail pit. An ornate wrought iron chandelier hung from the high ceiling. The addition of an old

Debbie by our pub bar

iron breastplate with crossed swords behind it over the fireplace finished off the living room, all that was left was the furnishings.

A guy I knew was an art director for United Artists. He told me that a movie director he knew had brought some drapes that had hung in an Italian palace over from Italy. They were for a house he had planned to build, but he had changed his mind and decided to build a modern style house instead. The drapes were too ornate for a modern house. He offered to practically give them away. I jumped on the deal but he didn't give them away. However I just about stole them!

When I showed them to a friend of mine who was a New York interior decorator. She saw that they contained real gold thread. She told me that the material they were made from would cost several hundred dollars a yard. They were just what I needed for the massive windows in the new room.

It took a lot of work to locate furniture that looked like it was from five centuries past. I found it in a catalog and ordered it. The ancient looking furniture was very uncomfortable but, that was ok as it was seldom used. We mostly sat in our huge conversation pit.

Our new living room was like no other. It looked like a Hollywood production!

The dinning room in our new house was very quaint just as it was. It had a nice old fireplace, wide planked floors and a beamed ceiling. A huge glass paneled window on one wall overlooked a small courtyard with a little pond and a fountain that I had constructed. Another wall had French doors at both ends. Between the french doors stood a big oak silver cabinet that looked very old but wasn't. I had designed it myself.

To add the finishing touches to this room I had a long heavy oak table made that looked like one I had seen in a Spanish castle. The table was surrounded by big ornate tall backed chairs that also looked like ones I had seen in Spain. The very last touch was supplied by a big wrought iron chandelier. I had designed that also and then had it made by an old blacksmith shop in nearby Norwalk, Connecticut.

Helen and I decided that our happiness would be enhanced if we

Our three level living room and our dining room

had a nice big swimming pool. We were, however, concerned about the cost. A pool builder was consulted. He agreed to build us a nice twenty by forty-foot gunite pool for a bargain price. He wanted to try an experiment. He wanted to see if he could build it under a big tent in January.

The contractor informed me that if he hit any rock that had to be dynamited it would add to the price. He also told me that he usually had to blast when building pools in Connecticut. New England is full of rocks and our house sat on huge granite boulders.

Then he further added to my fears that the cost could get out of hand. He informed me of the extra cost of a pool he had just finished. That pool for Elia Kazan, the great movie director, had required $40,000 (in 1960's money) extra for rock removal!

All this meant that if we hit rock our swimming pool would be washed down the drain. We would have to pay him for the work he had done and forget about a pool. I convinced Helen to let us buck the odds and plunge ahead.

The boomerang shaped pool was built into the side of a hill with a wide deck around it. The deck on the downward slope of the hill ended almost at tree top level and the effect was dramatic. It was built under a huge tent during the frigid days of a New England winter with the workman inside the tent mostly working shirtless.

Dumb luck prevailed. If the pool had been any other shape or even inches deeper, rock would have had to be blasted. The pool builder had been surprised when we went ahead with the project. Our luck amazed him. I am sure that he was pleased that his experiment in building a pool in midwinter had succeeded.

My next project was to landscape the pool and the areas around the house that were not forested. The large deck surrounding the pool and the walks required thousands of square feet of blue stone flagging. This was made affordable by cutting the cost from over five dollars a square foot to less than two dollars a square foot. The flagstones were purchased directly from the quarry in Vermont. Then I oversaw the laying of them myself. The necessity of having to mow grass was eliminated by covering the remaining area with snow white pea gravel. The white pea gravel was enhanced by islands of flowering greenery.

While all this work on the house and grounds was going on I had to keep turning out illustrations to pay for it and to support the family.

A small Norman-style guest cottage and an attached garage had come with the house. The guest cottage was used as a studio until a big studio could be built. The new studio building consisted of a three car garage at ground level with a studio above. The studio/garage building was positioned so that a drive-in court was formed.

My new garage/studio had to blend in with the other buildings. Such practical modern conveniences as overhead doors would not look right. The problem was solved by making the overhead doors look like old hinged doors. I got the overhead door company to custom make some doors from a drawing that I gave them. My doors looked just like old fashioned doors. It took quite a bit of effort for me to figure out how to make things separate properly when they folded though. The door company had to properly balance the doors because of their nonstandard thickness but they worked.

I made the ornate fake hinges out of masonite and they were painted black, but the fake latches in the middle of the doors presented a problem. They needed to have the top of a large bolt protruding from their middle. I could not cut out something that small with my saber saw. The weighty problem was solved by simply using bottle caps painted black.

The doors looked so good that word got around and now and then Architects came and asked to see them. Today ready-made overhead doors are available that look like they open like conventional doors. But there weren't any back then.

My studio was above the new garage

I had a problem getting masons to build walls that looked old and crudely constructed. When the wall that attached the studio to the guest cottage was constructed, I wanted it to have an old Gothic style gate in it that looked old and massive. Building things straight and as perfect as possible is ingrained in masons. They can't bring themselves to do otherwise. I repeatedly had to grab the trowel and demonstrate that a large degree of crudeness contributed to the look of a by gone age.

The completion of the new garage freed up the old garage. It was added to the guest cottage.

Our new digs now lacked only one thing, a dramatic kitchen. The kitchen was built on three levels like the living room. The top level was for cooking, the middle level was for eating and on the lowest level was another big conversation pit. Everything was designed so that Helen could have a clear view of the pool while she was cooking. She knew that the kids would spend a lot of time there and she wanted to keep an eye on them.

The kitchen windows overlooked the pool. They were much larger than they appear to be in this picture.

Two walls of the kitchen required very large windows. The windows had to support a lot of weight because of their size and they had to be metal because wood would not be strong enough. The problem was that there were no metal residential windows big enough. I discovered that there were factory windows of sufficient dimensions though, and that is what we used. Massive old beams salvaged from an old school house were the finishing touch. They were put up while the whole family was on a trip to the island of Antigua.

When we returned, the builders, who were old shipwrights from Maine, proudly showed me their work. They had done a good job on the kitchen except for one thing. They had used an adz to give the beams a hand-hewn look. Of course hand-adzed old beams were a much sought after item, but not when they looked like raw wood! The beautiful old patina of my ancient beams was totally gone. They were, however, already securely in place and not able to be removed.

I experimented with various mixtures of paint but nothing worked. Finally I climbed up on a big step ladder and went to work on them. I seared them with a blowtorch, keeping a fire extinguisher in my other hand. After I finished my beams then looked pretty good.

I should have known better than to leave the shipwrights from Maine unsupervised. Although they were master carpenters, they had a limited knowledge of what was required to make things look old.

They had been retained to remodel our guest cottage the winter before when it was too cold to work on boats in Maine. I had gone over to the guest cottage just in time to prevent them from tearing out all the paneling in the guest cottage living room. It was paneled with wormy cypress which is an expensive wood. It gets its charm from all the worm holes. They thought it was rotten wood!

Despite everything, the boat builders were superb craftsmen. I was lucky to have found them. Another discovery was Yanos, an energetic young yard worker from Hungary. He groomed our property and kept it looking shipshape.

Hungary had just been brought back under the Soviet yoke by Russian tanks. The poor people had experienced only a brief taste of freedom during the revolution. Yanos had been freed from a political prison when it was captured by the freedom fighters during the early days of the Hungarian Revolution.

Yanos had escaped from Hungary by crawling through a mine field while evading guards, dogs, barbed wire and searchlights. After gaining his freedom he had been torn by remorse over having to leave his mother in Hungary. He attempted to go back to bring her out, but his luck had run out. He was captured by the secret police and thrown in prison.

Janos was liberated from the prison by Hungarian revolutionaries during Hungary's brief period of freedom. Just before the revolution was

This was an illustration of an ambush of the Russian invaders during the Hungarian Revolution.

crushed, he simply walked across the boarder into Austria with his mother. From Austria Janos emigrated to the United States.

    Yanos saved his money and bought a truck and some equipment. Soon he had another truck and guy working for him. I told Helen that he was a man who would go far. I am sure that he did.

    Everything was now complete and we could settle into our new digs. I really enjoyed having a big studio away from everybody. The fact that it was up stairs above the garage gave it the feeling of privacy. I had the feeling that, even though I was near the house, I was in my own world. I am sure that Helen also enjoyed having me out of the house most of the day.

    The trip to Antigua we had been on while the new kitchen was constructed, had been brought about at the instigation of Helen's mother. "Meme," as she was affectionately called, invited the whole family on a trip to the beautiful island. Of course we readily accepted.

A delightful little resort called Hawk's Bill was our abode for the joyous weeks we spent there. It was named for a unique big rock that reared out of the ocean. The rock looked just like a giant hawk's head.

Our days were spent with beach activities and island explorations. Our evenings were spent drinking sweet rum drinks and competing in limbo contests and dancing.

One evening I met a very interesting guy in the bar at our resort. He was the owner and captain of a big yacht, The *Warrior Girante*. He did not have a charter for the next day. Because of this he offered to take us on a cruise to a nearby uninhabited island. We had only to pick up the tab for the fuel. Helen's brother, John, offered to pitch in and we readily accepted.

Early the next morning we were out on the dock waiting in the bright Caribbean sun. An awe inspiring apparition appeared. The *Warrior Girante* was a converted warship and over a hundred feet long. A launch was lowered and we were soon aboard the mighty leviathan. We began a never to be forgotten adventure.

The merry crew

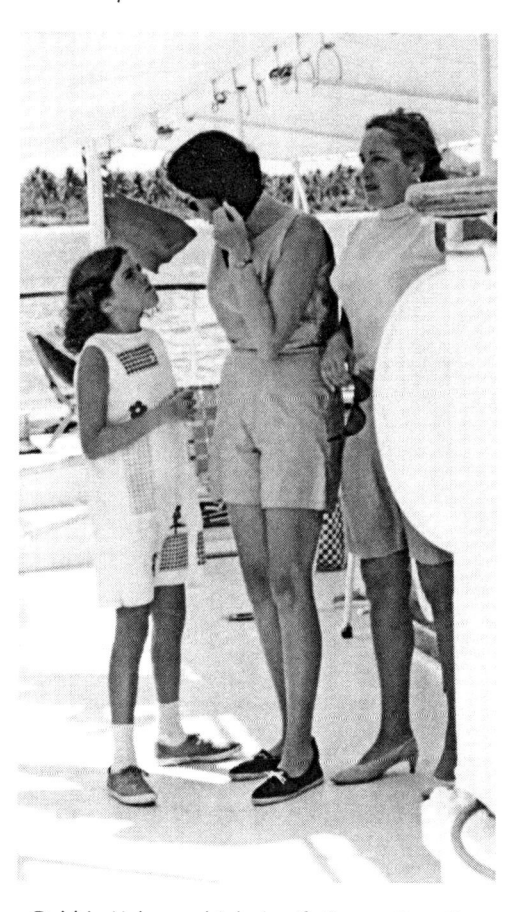

Debbie, Helen and John's wife Georgett on the *Warrior Girante*

An oil painting of Gary looking at fossils on a beach in Antigua

of the mighty "warrior" largely consisted of some pretty young airline stewardesses and Oxford University students. To our further delight a well stocked bar awaited us. As if this was not enough, our rugged, bearded captain announced that he had served as an officer in the Royal Indian Navy in WW II. After the war he had graduated from the Cordon Bleu in Paris. Our bearded host prepared an Indian feast for us worthy of a Maharajah.

The curry we experienced that day was truly memorable. The varied dishes of chutney could be counted by the dozen. Alas, I took too great an advantage of the prodigious offerings of the well stocked bar. My memories of the glorious cruise are seriously blurred.

Another time, John went out sailing on a tiny boat. The sail broke free and he was being swept out to sea by the current. Earlier, we had been informed that there were a lot of sharks out beyond the reef. To our distress he was headed there. Fortunately, I noticed his predicament and managed to swim out to help him in just in time. It took both of us swimming as hard as we could to get John and the boat safely back to shore.

Antigua was great fun except for one other unpleasant experience. The island was having a water shortage. The water was shut off after a certain time each night, because of this, I saved a glass of water for brushing my teeth.

One night after returning to the room, feeling green in the gills, I mistakenly attempted to brush my teeth with hair gel. In that time men groomed their hair with a hair tonic that was a gel, mine came in a tube that was the same color as my toothpaste. As I abruptly reacted to the taste of the hair jel I accidentally knocked over the glass of water.

A night spent sick as a dog with a mouth full of hair tonic and no water was a night of pure torture.

Once again we returned from the islands and resumed our normal routines. I got to work and brought our finances back into shape. Freelancing is a feast or famine existence. I insisted that the only money that could be borrowed was the original mortgage on our house. Everything else had to be paid for as we went along. This included the additions we had made to our house and surrounding property. Our budget had been strained but I was able to pull us through. Helen had some money but my pride would not allow us to use it. I always considered it my duty to support the family.

Helen always handled all our financial affairs. If we needed to buy something such as a car she would tell me if we had enough money or not. We usually had a couple of cars, one of them was almost always a snappy sports car. Helen didn't like sports cars but she never objected to my owning one. She drew the line at me letting the top down when she rode with me though. She hated convertibles because the wind messed her hair.

Helen and I decided that it was time that we took the family on a trip around the United States. Helen wanted her children to be exposed to as much of the world as possible, so she set to work planning a route. I was always too busy working to spend time planning trips and I knew that she would do an excellent job. Other than the final destination, I rarely knew where we were going, I just followed, her directions.

Our trip was more than eleven thousand miles, which is almost half way around the world. It took us eight weeks. We went through the southwest and reached California just south of Los Angeles. Our journey took us up the entire west coast to Victoria in British Columbia. Then we drove east and reentered the United States through Glacier National Park.

We traveled in a Lincoln Continental convertible that was one of the last four door convertibles made. The top took up most of the trunk when it went down. With all the luggage we had to carry we couldn't put it down the entire trip. Helen would not have allowed me to put it down in any case, as I said before, she would never ride with the top down.

The huge trunk lid could only be raised electronically, which caused a miserable visit in Las Vegas. When we arrived there it was blast furnace hot. I had experienced a lot of deep south summers but nothing

Our car that had a trunk lid on strike

like this. It was over one hundred degrees at night.

Our car trunk had decided to go on strike. Nothing we could do would cajole it to open, and every place of aid was closed. We had to go into the big hotel drenched in perspiration, and toothbrushless. This incident probably contributed to my dislike of Vegas. I forgave the car though, and I wish I had it back.

I had never liked the work of Charles Russell, the famous western painter and illustrator. I thought his color too garish. But my mind was abruptly changed when I saw the color of western landscapes in the late afternoon. I could hardly believe it when I first beheld the spectrum orange on a section of a butte in the bright light and also the spectrum purple in the shadowed areas. Charles Russell was right!

We visited his studio in Great Falls, Montana and saw beautiful miniature sculptures of his in the Montana state capitol at Helena. I had not known that he was also a sculptor. His tiny three dimensional work was truly remarkable.

As the story goes, Mr. Russell once formed a beautiful little bear out of a big wad of clay while having a drink at a bar. One of the bar customers asked him what he would take for the bear. After Charles Russell said "Ten dollars," the man offered him five.

Mr.. Russell without hesitation, smashed the bear back into a lump of clay and broke it into two pieces. He then calmly fashioned one half into a bear and sold it to the man for five dollars.

One of my closest friends, Tom Lovell, used sculptures that he created as models for some of his illustrations. When he did a series of illustrations for a *National Geographic Magazine* article about Alexander the Great, he sculpted a terrific battle elephant. He used it as a model in the illustration that depicted charging elephants in a battle scene in India.

Tom built many excellent models for his work. He constructed a model of a Viking ship to be used for another *National Geographic* story. This led to a discovery that changed a part of history. Tom discovered that the way historians had thought sails on Viking ships worked was wrong. I believe his series of illustrations depicting the Vikings were some of the best ever done.

In Virginia City, Montana we met an old lady. The lady told us she was from back when it had been a thriving silver mining town. She said that in the old days it could cost you your life if you left town. Bandits lay in wait in areas around the town. It was not enough for them to just put a bandana over their nose and mouth as in the Hollywood westerns. She said that people could be recognized by their horse. They either had to cover the horse or kill you. She said most of the time they just killed you!

Illustrator down to his last brushes after a long siege —

Tom Lovell celebrating the completion of his *Alexander* illustrations for *National Geographic Magazine*

We had seen a number of antelope as we progressed across the west but we had not seen any buffalo. Helen assured me that we would see some buffalo when we got to Custer National Park.

We arrived at Custer National Park and we saw lots of grassland and the Little Big Horn River where Custer met his demise, but we had not seen a single buffalo.

I spotted a wooded area and got out of the car to answer a call of nature in the woods. As I was answering the call, I heard a noise and looked up. I was staring directly into the eyes of a monster. It was the

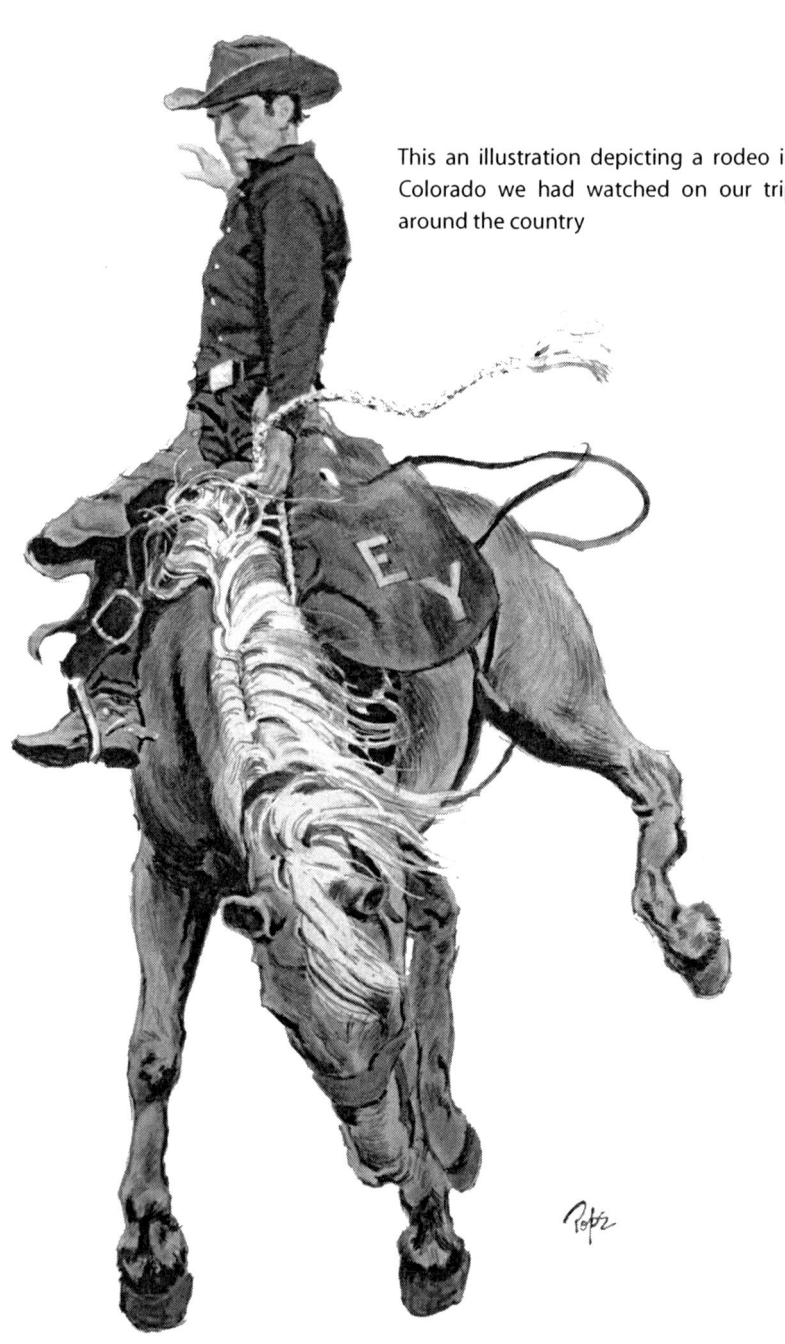

This an illustration depicting a rodeo in Colorado we had watched on our trip around the country

biggest bull buffalo I have ever seen. The woods were full of buffalo!

Nature's answer was cut short and a hasty retreat was made. I learned that buffalo don't spend all their time out on the grass.

After eight weeks on the road, we'd had quite a few adventures and a lot of good times. And after much newly-acquired knowledge about our country, our little family arrived back in Westport.

By the 1960s book publishers had begun to pay halfway decent money for elementary level text book illustrations. I had discovered that illustrating them offered some advantages: there was very little deadline pressure; the trips to the city were far apart, and the time allotted to illustrating an entire book was several months. Of course I did other work which required trips to town. I didn't, however, have to go as often as I once did.

I always disliked having to spend time picking up and delivering jobs. More and more I gravitated toward book illustration. It allowed me to spend more time illustrating and less time running around.

As a result of our western trip, Helen and I had gotten interested in the Pueblo Indians. When we visited the Great Pueblo in Taos, New Mexico I was afforded the privilege of an invitation to visit an Indian family's apartment inside the pueblo. The inside of the Great Pueblo is normally off limit to non Indians.

The Taos Pueblo is made out of mud bricks and is well over eight hundred years old. This ancient building is much as it was when Coronado visited it in 1540.

At the entrance to the pueblo area a young Pueblo Indian on duty at the gate had noticed a sticker on our car's windshield. It identified us as residents of Westport. He announced that he was a student of the Famous Artists School, an art correspondence school in Westport. When he asked me what I did and was told that I was an illustrator he invited me to visit

An illustration I did depicting Coronado at Taos

his home in the pueblo.

The building was ancient but inside the Indians had all the modern conveniences save television. In those days television required an aerial. The tribe forbad anything modern on the outside of the pueblo.

The Pueblos are the only tribe of Indians whose culture has not been largely destroyed by the white race. They have churches but they also have kivas, places of worship for their old religion.

Helen and I became very interested in the Pueblos and the Anasazi, the ancestral Pueblos, after visiting other pueblos and their ancient cliff dwellings. We heard that one pueblo was very different from all the others. It had a square kiva. This was very unusual because all the many other kivas in the many other pueblos are round. Even though, San Carlos, the pueblo with the square kiva was far off our route we decided to visit it.

After a long drive on a hot dusty road, we arrived at the pueblo. It seemed deserted because even though there was clear evidence of current human activity, there was no one to be seen. Everything was so eerie that

Helen and the kids wouldn't get out of the car.

Kivas are adobe buildings with no doors or windows just a hole in the top. A notched pole protrudes from the hole allowing access to the kiva's interior.

I got out of the car and started to climb the stairs which led to the top of the kiva. I knew that this was a no no. But no one was around and I possess a prodigious curiosity. As I began to ascend the stairs I suddenly underwent an extremely painful event. I had experienced the same thing the year before, back in Westport. I had been attacked by a swarm of yellow jackets and had to dive into our pool fully clad, to escape them. This time, on reflection, I didn't actually see yellow jackets, but it felt as if my pants were full of them and they were stinging me all over my body, and the pain was severe.

In agony, I panicked and raced for the car. I jumped in and we sped off. The pain instantly vanished. There were no yellow jackets. It had all been in my mind! This was the strangest experience of my life and I can't explain it.

Soon after returning to Westport I decided to put all our newfound knowledge to good use in the form of two books. I had no confidence in my writing ability but I had complete confidence in Helen's writing ability. She embraced my ideas for the books and agreed to apply her talent to the project.

One book was the story of the Anasazi and Pueblo people. The other book was a simple history of the United States as viewed from a Spanish viewpoint.

We set to work producing an outline and a sample chapter for each book. I also did some finished comp illustrations for each book.

I took the work we had done to one of the senior editors at Holt, Rinehart and Winston in New York. The path to his door was paved for me by an art director at Holt for whom I had illustrated a book.

Our timing on this project was perfect. Multi-ethnic culture was the hottest game in town for educational publishers. When he saw the oldest public document in the U.S, a Florida marriage contract in Spanish from the 1500s. and the governor's palace in Santa Fe, New Mexico is our oldest public building, his eyes lit up. And when I laid a map of the United States with all the Spanish names printed in red in front of him his eyes almost popped. Practically the whole western United States would be red!

At this time anything positive about Indians or Hispanics was pure gold in the eyes of publishers. We had two winners!

The editor offered to buy the books outright and he offered me a lot of money. He said that he wanted to base a series of books on them. The offer was attractive. I took it subject to one condition which he readily accepted. The condition was that I got to illustrate any and all of the books if I chose to do so.

Perhaps I could have made an even better deal but I felt we were well paid for our efforts, and we were spared a lot of work. I could now settle down and get on with new endeavors.

One not so minor benefit of our book projects was that we could legitimately deduct a sizable portion of our western adventure from our income tax.

After settling down and working for the fall and winter months I was once again subjected to Helen's wanderlust. She had decided that we should spend the approaching summer on the coast of Spain. Westport was one of the top "In" places for wealthy New Yorkers in the summer. Our house was very popular with movie people because we had a pool. Also because it was private and unusual. We rented it several summers to movie directors. They paid enormous rents and Spain in those days was dirt-cheap.

España

Helen rented a house for us on the coast of Spain in a town I had never heard of, called Benidorm, we surrendered our house keys to our rental agent and took wing to Spain, via France.

Helen had purchased a new Volkswagen square back, which we picked up in Paris. Our family fit very comfortably in the little car. We promptly headed for San Sebastian on the Bay of Bisque just over the Pyrenees in Spain.

We arrived at our hotel in San Sebastian after dark. There we were greeted with bad news. The reservationist at the hotel informed us that they had not received our reservation. He further informed us that they were completely booked. To make matters even worse, just about every room in the city was taken. The San Sebastian Film Festival, second only to the Cannes Film Festival in importance, was taking place.

At the time I could not understand why they had not received our reservation. I knew that Helen was always careful to make hotel reservations for our first and last nights on foreign trips. Later it dawned on me that in many countries peoples' last names appear first on lists and forms. We had told them that we had a reservation in the name of Pope. When we were told we had no reservation, we should have asked them if they had a reservation in the name of Miller! In any event, our failure to obtain a room in that first class hotel led to a memorable visit to San Sebastian. The man on the front desk, who had given us the bad news about our reservation, told us that there were a couple of vacant rooms at a little third-class hotel across town. At this point we were glad to get anything. The kind Spaniard called the hotel for us and gave us directions to get there.

The hotel sat up on a high cliff and at one time had been a very large house. We had to lug our luggage up a flight of stairs and our rooms had no private bath. But they were large, clean and comfortable even though the furniture had witnessed better days. We had to walk down the hall to the large bathroom but we counted ourselves lucky to have a place to sleep.

Our fortunes took a turn for the better when we went down stairs for dinner. The evening turned into a party because the dining room was full of boys from Yale. They were on their way home from Pamplona where they had participated in the Running of the Bulls. They were celebrating their escape from the horns of the angry bovines.

Helen was an attractive young American woman and we were almost as young as the Yalies. That fact and one other made a huge contribution to our frivolity. In Spain, pitchers of the local wine were included in the price of dinner. The kids went up to bed and we were left with the memory of a wonderful night in San Sebastian.

We left San Sebastian and had the usual tourist adventures as we traversed Spain. It was very hot as we traveled across Castile. We passed an old Christian castle with an old Moorish castle in the far distance. I remember thinking how miserable it was to have been a knight during the Reconquista. They would not have dared to wander into such a no man's land without wearing all their armor. Knights wore heavy felt under their armor to prevent chaffing. The heavy felt combined with the encasing metal must have created a furnace effect. They must have been miserable.

We experienced the sights and sounds of Burgos, Toledo and Madrid. Once again we got to dine where Hemmingway had dined. This necessitated a trip to Segovia to feast on roast suckling pig in one of Hemmingway's favorite haunts. This time around, I encountered the unpleasant experience that I related earlier.

A vast amount of Spanish wine was not sufficient to overcome my squeamishness upon encountering a tiny ear attached to my entree. I never again ate roast suckling pig.

It was very late in the afternoon when we arrived in Seville. The guide at the famous Alcazar of Seville complained that his feet hurt too much to take us on a final tour of the day. I told him I remembered how much his feet had hurt him a few years before, he had taken Helen and me on the same tour. He remembered us and relented. It was the only opportunity we had to expose the kids to the historic place. We were on a tight schedule to traverse Spain, then to cross over the Mediterranean to Tangier in Morocco. Then, after a few days in North Africa to recross the Mediterranean to Spain.

When we arrived in Tangier I discovered that Helen had booked us into a different hotel than the one we had stayed in on our earlier trip to Tangier. When we arrived we encountered our second occasion of a lost reservation, we were fortunate to find accommodations in a another nearby hotel.

On this trip to Morocco we lacked the services of Mohammed, whose guide services we had employed on the prior visit. We encountered another Mohammed on our walk along the Tangier waterfront. He offered his services as a guide. The new Mohammed was a cute little lad of tender years. He spoke a lot of languages and seemed to be very smart. The kids insisted on his employment and his services were duly engaged.

Mohammed did a good job but he had to be careful. If the regular guides caught him acting as a guide he would be severely beaten. We had invited him to have a coke with us in the hotel garden bar but he was afraid. We insisted and he relented because a Coca-Cola was something very special and expensive to a poor kid like Mohammed. Our waiter was very displeased to see him with us but he got the Coke.

I needed to buy a small tote bag and since I didn't speak Arabic I asked Mohammed to translate. He told me that all the merchants were

Helen and the kids in Tangier with Mohammed, our diminutive guide

thieves and that they would ask too much. I followed his instructions to the letter. I bought the bag for a fraction of the original price asked by the merchant.

The transaction was interesting. First he had me ask the price. Upon receiving it, I marked half as much on the merchant's pad. The merchant marked a new sum on the pad. I countered with yet a new sum and the merchant shook his head. Then, as little Mohammed had instructed, I turned and began to walk away. The merchant followed and accepted my sum just as Mohammed had predicted he would.

I told Helen that if that kid ever came to the United States he would end up as a rich man.

We left little Mohammed as he did not dare go to the boat with us. We had to leave him blocks away.

The boat from North Africa docked at Algiciras. We picked up our little VW square back. Then we drove up the Spanish Coast to

Alicante to meet a plane from the States. Helen's mother and her friend, Kay Bell, were arriving from the United States for a visit.

We made it to the airport in Alicante in time and picked them up. Then we resumed our journey up the Costa Blanca (White Coast) to Benidorm.

The house in Benidorm Helen had rented, vastly exceeded our expectations. It was a large house that sat on top of a hill. The house had its own private beach and overlooked the town and a broad expanse of the Mediterranean. It had spacious grounds which were protected by a beautiful wrought iron fence. The drive to the house was through massive wrought iron gates and as one approached the house, there was a beautiful view of the sea through the stately trees. Often a Spanish policeman with his distinctive flat leather hat stood guard by the wall that surrounded the property.

Our Spanish abode was straight out of a movie. In fact, it literally

The view from one of the terraces of our house in Benedorm

was, only it had been an English movie. I saw the movie once on TV. I didn't see the beginning so I never knew the title. It starred the great English actor Jack Hawkins who died from throat cancer. In the movie he was a great international bad guy. Our house was his lair. The inside of the house was different, but outside it was our rental house in all its Spanish splendor. The house was called El Raco for some reason. As far as I know it doesn't mean anything in Spanish.

The long summer days spent at El Raco in Benidorm were pleasant and mostly uneventful. Juana, our Spanish, cook, prepared delicious Spanish culinary delights. We had our own little beach to swim from. We had two terraces with magnificent views for cocktails, and our house was very roomy and comfortable.

One day I decided to drive to Denia. I had read that there was a Moorish castle there. I love old castles. It was perfect and I had it all to myself. It was the first time that I was ever able to wonder around an ancient castle without an escort. It became apparent to me that the castle on the hilltop was not the hilltops' first occupant. There were clues that it had been occupied by a Greek temple in more ancient times. This was revealed by a number of remnants from Greek columns used by the Moors in the castle's walls. My conclusion was confirmed when I later read that the castle did indeed occupy the site of a former Greek temple.

A deviation from our bucolic routine at El Raco occurred when the Volkswagen needed some servicing. This would deprive us of its services for a couple of days. Rather than be afoot for the period, we rented a Siat. We decided to drive to Granada and visit the Alhambra. The Siat was roomy enough for four adults and two kids. but it overheated and broke down on the way back. There was a farmhouse nearby and the people who lived there tried to help us. They were very poor and it was apparent that they had very little water. The area was very arid but they filled our radiator with their precious water. They were too proud to accept

This picture of Gary and Debra posing as Moors was taken by a photographer in the Alhambra in Granada

Helen and Gary on one of EL Raco's terraces

any payment and would not relent despite my insistence.

Unfortunately the generosity of those poor people was to no avail. I shall however, always remember the kindness of the Spanish people. Our rescue had to await the Spanish police who got us back to Grenada. A new problem awaited us at the car rental office in Grenada. The only car they had was a tiny Simca. I was determined to get us back to Benidorm. Six of us had to cram into a car that would normally not hold four people comfortably. It was a long miserable drive but we finally made it back to our house.

Our balmy days in El Raco finally came to an end. We put Meme and her friend on a plane in Alicante and resumed our jaunty journey. The little Volkswagen station wagon carried us down the Costa Brava through

Barcelona and into France. After mostly happy adventures traversing France our little band arrived on the English Channel.

The one unhappy culinary adventure for me was in Dijon, other than the "little ear" of course.

One of the great Michelin three star restaurants was there. Helen had announced that we had to go through Dijon. It was the culinary capitol of the world, so of course we had to dine in the best restaurant there. As I have noted before, the one great exception to her frugality was wining and dining.

My pleading for pocketbook mercy was to no avail. There were four of us and I feared that the tab might equal the national debt. It almost did!

The table was huge and Helen sat far from me with the kids in-between. The French had no mercy for hicks from the sticks like me. Only French was spoken and printed on the menu. The menu was the size of a newspaper and only mine had prices on it.

The remainder of the family could not see how whatever they ordered would contribute to our financial ruin. The sommelier with his little silver cup was especially intimidating since I, as a peasant, had no knowledge of French wines. Beer was my speed.

The waiter did not leave the table as long as the menu was being studied. Helen spoke perfect upper class French and was born to take situations like this in stride. But she was fully occupied translating for Debbie and Gary. She was, in any case too far away to help me in my acute distress.

Too add to my misery, I knew that the French eat some pretty weird stuff, such as snails, rabbits and blood pudding. Helen ate that stuff, but not me. I could not even eat a lobster.

The word poulet on the menu was recognized and I knew that it meant chicken. I ordered that and prayed that it was a normal part of the chicken.

When one remembers that I was in the Marine Corps. One has to wonder what I would have done in some kind of survival situation. Would I have eaten bugs or would I have starved? As silly as my squeamishness is, after all protein is protein, I can't change. I still can't pick up a bug.

After Dijon we resumed our once again happy jaunt across the beautiful French countryside, albeit with a flattened wallet to Dieppe!

From Dieppe we joined the Volkswagen on a boat trip across the channel to Dover.

We drove away from Dover and headed down the English Coast. Debbie voiced her impression of England. "It's so cute!" she squealed.

Our first night was spent at a little inn in Alfredston. Alfredston is right out of a Charles Dickens novel. The perfect place to spend a Christmas.

The inn, Ye Olde Smuggler's Inn was built in the fourteenth century and exuded atmosphere. There were only three guest rooms in

Debra and Gary in *Little*

the inn. They were arranged around a small living room all on the second floor. We occupied them all. Debra slept in one tiny room which bore the title Little. Gary slept in a slightly larger room entitled Slanting. His aptly named room's floor slanted downward. It required wooden blocks to keep the bed from rolling downhill. I don't remember the name of our third room, but I'm sure it was equally quaint. The wattle walls of the ancient establishment leaned outward at a serious angle. However the warm fire in the quaint little fireplace in the living room and the extreme charm of the old place more than compensated for any inconveniences we encountered.

Helen washed out a few items of clothing and I went downstairs to the bar. The bar reminded me of an old English pub in the cinema. It had everything that I had expected to see except a dart board. My disappointment was soon dissipated. A cabinet on the wall was opened to reveal a proper English dart board. The habitués then began to compete for drinks.

I struck up a conversation with two old blokes who were former Royal Marines. I asked them which ship they had served on and they told me the *Ajax*. I told them that I was a former U.S. Marine. I also revealed that I Knew the history of how the cruisers *Ajax* and *Achilles* had bagged the mighty battleship *Graff Spee*. After that I was never allowed to buy another drink!

The next morning we were off to Battle near Hastings to visit the site of the epic battle. The battle determined whether England would be mostly linked in the future to Europe, or linked to Scandinavia. After visiting Battle we proceeded across England to London. After more adventures we winged our way home.

When we returned we found our house in pristine condition. I was told the movie director who had rented it had only been able to use it for one week, then his servant or servants had nothing to do but primp the house and grounds. It had never looked better!

I got back to work to reinflate our wallet.

American Airlines was planning to introduce their new jumbo jets, which they had just purchased. The agency employed to prepare the ads had in turn employed a top interior design illustrator. His assignment was to picture the proposed interior of the new planes. He did not do people so I was contacted by an artist rep to populate the plane's interior. The ad would consist of one large illustration and two smaller ones. They would fill a two page spread in magazines and newspapers all across the country.

The money was good but not the time frame. I was contacted on Thursday. The art had to be in the hands of the agency by nine A.M. the following Monday. I considered this to be an almost impossible task. I tried to turn it down, but each time I was offered more money, I finally could not refuse.

The guy doing the interiors lived over in Norwalk, next to Westport. As soon as he had penciled a tissue (A kind of tracing paper) of one of the interior illustrations, the rep who was standing by would bring it to me. I penciled in the people in the plane while the interior guy worked on the next tissue.

When all the pencils were done the same process was repeated with the finishes. The rep got the final illustration from me on Sunday night. When I gave it to him I was so bleary eyed from lack of sleep that I didn't know whether I had created an abortion, a master piece or something in between.

The rep called me on Monday afternoon. I was happy to hear that they liked the job. However, they were not going to use it. The airline board felt that "It committed them." They had Peter Arno the famous New Yorker cartoonist do a cartoon. Arno's cartoons wouldn't commit anyone to anything. I didn't care because I got a big fat check for my lack of sleep.

On a number of other occasions I got commissions to put people into things, mostly autos. Objects like automobiles in ads were usually not photos. They were air brush illustrations done by commercial still life illustrators. These were the days when bigger was better. Before the advent of computer graphics it was much harder to make photographs lie.

In many automobile ads air brush illustrations supplied the answer. A good commercial still life illustrator could stretch out the car. He could make it appear much longer than it really was and he could make the vast expanses of chrome on cars shine better than in reality. The only problem was that they couldn't draw people. That's where guys like me came in.

A problem arose when the illustrator doing the auto rendered it from an angle that made it very difficult to insert people into the car properly. I remember one job that required me to put a couple into a new Saab. It was rendered from a slightly overhead angle that would require the insertion of midgets. Otherwise their heads would not show.

I somehow solved the problem and saved the job. I honestly can't remember how I did it. I remember that job, but not because of the illustration problem. I remember it because of what happened when I delivered the job very late one Friday afternoon.

The agency art director on the account was siting around with an old gentleman. They were having an end-of-the-day drink. Agency brass frequently had a bar set up in their offices in those days. He invited me to have a drink, to relax and join them. I eagerly accepted the kind invitation and entered into a conversation that I have always remembered.

The old man had been involved in early radio. He had some fascinating stories to relate. He had been with an agency in Chicago or Detroit, I can't remember which. A man made a presentation to the agency for a new radio show. The agency had a client, Merita Bread, as I recall, that was in need of a program to sponsor.

The guy making the presentation asked for seventy-five dollars a week to write each weekly episode and produce it. His idea was about a masked cowboy with an Indian sidekick named Tonto. You guessed it. *The Lone Ranger!* The agency decided to go for it and it was an instant hit.

After the year's contract was up the creator of the big hit was called in to sign a new contract. He was told that the agency was going to give him a raise to one hundred dollars a week. The *Lone Ranger's* creator demanded one hundred and twenty-five dollars a week. He got it.

Another great story the old radio man related that evening concerned the first appearance of *Fibber McGee and Molly*, two of the most famous radio comedians in history. They first appeared on one of the earliest programs on one of the first stations. The program was simply the dinner conversation of a bunch of interesting people as they ate their evening meal. It took place back during the great depression. Their pay was the dinner!

Yet another story he related was about one of the most popular radio serials of all time, *Jack Armstrong, The All American Boy*. Each fifteen-minute episode was recorded on hard wax discs. They were sent out all over the country to be played for each weekday program. Unlike today, they could not be edited and patched. The cast had to record for the entire fifteen minutes without making a single mistake. This was a very difficult task. Each episode had to be recorded over and over seemingly endlessly until it was without any mistakes. The recordings were made on the top floor of a building in Chicago before there was air conditioning. If Jack and his companions were up in the Arctic, in the script, the sweltering crew in Chicago must have had their acting skills challenged.

I will always fondly recall the time listening to that old gentleman relating his stories of the early days of radio as we relaxed over our drinks. Radio provided a lot of enjoyment to most peoples lives before television.

Milestones

Soon after that occasion, I was invited to go on a "civilian orientation tour" by the secretary of the navy. The naval commander who was assigned to choose the "VIPs" for the trip was a friend. I am sure that fact played more than a minor part in my selection.

At work in my new studio

The trip originated at Floyd Bennett Field in Brooklyn New York. It was aboard a U.S. Navy transport aircraft equipped with all the comforts. Other than myself, all the other passengers were college presidents and C.E.O.s of big corporations. We were charged fifty dollars for what turned out to be a lavish three-day outing at the Pensacola Naval Air Station in Florida. We were also treated to a short cruise aboard the aircraft carrier U.S.S. *Lexington*, to observe practice trainee airplane landings.

The fifty dollars was the bare cost of our food so that the trip would, in theory, be of no cost to the taxpayers. It was explained to us that the pilot and the crew of the plane that transported us were getting in their airtime. The cost of our booze and such was paid for out of the officer's club profits.

We were housed in the bachelor officers quarters which were double rooms and not as lavish as the entertainment we were provided by the base.

At sea on the *Lexington*

A UNITED STATES NAVY PHOTOGRAPH

In the pilot's seat

I was astonished to wake up my first morning and find my bigwig roommate in the corner standing on his head with only a towel for padding practicing yoga!

It is still a mystery to me what benefit the U.S. Navy gained from my participation in the trip, but I enjoyed it.

Several years later I went on another trip as a guest of the United States Air Force to view the Air Force Museum at the Wright Paterson Air Force Base in Dayton, Ohio. The Navy quarters paled in comparison to the spacious suites that housed Air Force guests. I wondered why the Air Force squandered so much on their guests. That was until I found out that these lavish digs were where members of congress were "Parked" while being courted by the Air Force brass.

About this time, along with Helen's family, I was invited to a ceremony at Princeton University by the University. The ceremony was to induct Helen's great uncle, posthumously, into the Football Hall of Fame, her uncle, Big Bill Edwards, Had been Princeton's greatest player.

Helen's brother, John, showed us around. He had attended Princeton

Helen and the kids with their Uncle John and Aunt Georgette at Princeton

as well as her father and all her direct male relations for generations.

John had everything going for him, he was handsome, well educated, very smart and witty, but demon alcohol, did him in.

Helen's father had set up a scholarship which would have paid for Gary to go there, but Gary, refused to go to college. He wanted to be a rock musician.

A portrait of Teenage Gary by my friend, Ward Brackett

I was not in a position to push very hard because he knew that I had not been very fond of formal education myself. Tough love was administered when Gary went forth to seek his fortune among the high amps. I told him that I was not fond of his choice for a profession and that I would not finance it. I did tell him however, that I would always send him money to come home. To Gary's credit he never asked for any money even though he had some very tough times.

Gary was, and still is very bright, but he was what the schools call a chronic underachiever. Poor Helen tried everything she knew to get Gary achieving. Westport had some of the finest public schools in the country but, in desperation, she had Gary in and out of one private school after another.

Debbie at Abbot, now Phillips Andover

Gary has turned out to be an achiever after all. This, despite the fact that I was always too busy working or partying to be the father that I should have been.

Helen's mother, Meme, felt that Debra should attend one of the nation's finest private high schools. I felt that this was a waste of money. We supported an outstanding public high school with our taxes in Westport. Of course I lost the battle when Helen supported her mother in the matter.

Abbot, Meme's old alma mater was selected. Helen had not liked Emma Willard, an equally prestigious school, her old alma mater.

A number of years ago Abbot merged into its equally highfalutin' neighboring boys school, Phillips Andover Academy. Abbot, which was the nation's oldest girls school is no more. The trouble with Abbot, other than the staggering cost, was that almost all the girls except Debra were from big rich families or on scholarships for the poverty stricken. She was about the only middle class girl there.

At Debra's graduation we were subjected to a speech by one of the graduating girls. She droned on about how materialistic all their parents were and how they, their generation, disdained materialism.

Following the graduation I witnessed a deluge of materialism being loaded into station wagons and automobiles. The vast wealth of material was in the form of record players, televisions, radios, filled trunks and suitcases, and so on.

It seems to me that the more snobbish the school, the more liberal it was. I had sent a perfectly nice young lady to Abbot and I got back a girl who was on the verge of becoming a hippie.

Debby had a boyfriend who was a good-looking louse in my opinion. He had earned my disdain by going over to the yacht club where our sailboat was moored and taking it out without our permission. Debra wanted to go to the college where he was going.

This time I put my foot down and ordained her college destination.

Her graduation from Abbot occurred during the period when centers of higher learning were instituting coed dorms. There was no way that I would permit my daughter to live in a coed dorm.

I knew of one school that was still fairly straight-laced. My parents had lived in Clemson, South Carolina, and I was very familiar with the university there.

The university owned the tens of thousands of acres surrounding it. It also owned Clemson, the little college town next to it. The town of Clemson had been selected by the *New York Times Magazine* as one of the ten most beautiful towns in America. It had been founded by John C. Calhoun as a land grant school thus its vast acreage. For most of Clemson's existence it had been a military school for boys. Some of the strict military aspect still remained. Females were required to be back in their dorm by eleven P.M. There were no coed dorms.

Clemson had a very welcoming admissions policy but anyone

who failed to maintain a C average was booted out at the end of the first semester.

Debra got mad over the discussion about where she was going to college and smashed a wine glass in the kitchen sink. That did it! I told her that she was going to Clemson! I told her that if she behaved and maintained a C average she could go wherever she wanted after the first semester. Debra had always made good grades in all top schools. She was smart and she knew it. She knew I meant business and agreed to go, but snarled "After the first semester I'll blast out of that Podunk school."

Helen adjusting Debbie's bridal gown

Debra stayed on at Clemson until she graduated. Helen and I had sent Clemson a girl on the verge of hippiedom. Clemson sent us back a properly mannered young lady.

She had met Robert McCall, a very talented young man at Clemson and soon after she returned home, they were married. Bob became an outstanding architect and fathered two smart, beautiful grandchildren but the marriage only lasted a few years.

During the time our children were in school, I did a great geal of illustration for elementary school textbooks. The money was not as good as for magazine and advertising illustration. That fact was offset by the more relaxed pressure, the bigger volume of work, and the vastly reduced time schedule. This allowed enough room to fit in the more lucrative ad and magazine jobs.

For some reason, I ended up illustrating several elementary science text books for a number of publishers. I had taken no science in school. I was asked by Addison and Wesley, a major publisher, to illustrate their first grade science book.

I wanted the book to be something "New." To that end I convinced the art director and the editor in charge of the science series to let us break all the rules of book design. Books had always followed an overall design pattern. Margins, type sizes, fonts, etc. were uniform throughout the book. My idea was that we cover each lesson on a two-page spread. Each spread would be a surprise when the student turned the page. My idea was that this would help keep the student's interest up. We pulled out all the stops. We used every gimmick that could be conceived. We had pages that ran from rebuses to "Big foot" comic strips. And we did this without losing sight of the fact that we were teaching science. To give one example, I did the background for a spread about wind power by blowing colored dyes around using a straw. This was noted in the teachers work book. The teacher could point this out to the students as a use of wind power.

This first book led to the series becoming the number one selling science series in the country. It was translated into Spanish for Puerto Rico, and French for the providence of Quebec.

One bright Saturday morning as I was nearing the completion of the first book I heard a car drive up. It stopped under the window of my studio over the garage. Opening a window and looking down I was surprised to see Vence Bowman. He was the head art director for a major publisher. Vence had been the conductor on one of the best "Gravy trains" I had ever ridden on.

The "Gravy train" was said to be the largest illustration project ever undertaken at that time. It consisted of the complete revamping of *The Book of Knowledge* encyclopedia. The new encyclopedia had thousands and

The party life at 40 Valley Road was in keeping with the Westport lifestyle

Pool partys

thousands of pages of new illustrations and photos. When I had delivered a batch of illustrations I was invited to select as many new assignments as I thought I could handle in a reasonable time. Any expenses or time spent on research was paid by the publisher. Helen did a lot of research for me and she also did all the billing. We made a lot of money off the project. The bills were never questioned because we didn't get too greedy, but a "Gravy train" it was until the project was finished.

After calling out a good morning greeting, Vence announced the purpose of his visit. "Were you serious about what you were talking about last night?", he asked.

The question left me at a loss for words. I didn't have the slightest idea of what he was talking about. As I remember, I answered, "Vence I'm always serious about what I'm talking about." This answer was a ploy to gain time to recall what I must have said. Fortunately after a moment of stunned silence, it dawned on me what he was talking about.

The preceding Friday night had been the night we had attended the monthly dinner and show at The Westport Artists meeting. As was all too frequently the case in those days, I had invited any who wished the revelry to continue to convene back at my house. Vence was very fond of the sauce and had been one of the continuing revelers.

As the clock crept into the wee hours and most had crept off to their warm beds Vence had soldiered on. I had related to him an idea I had for saving a lot of money in book publishing. The whole thing would have died right there if he had not liked the idea so much. I am good at thinking things up, but very poor at carrying them out.

A idea had dawned on me one day when I was delivering a job to a very big publisher at their fancy offices on Madison Avenue. I wondered how much money could be saved putting books together by moving out of such stratospherically costly digs and putting it all under one roof.

Executives and creative people in the industry for the most part come in from the burbs around nine. Around ten thirty work stopped for a coffee and Danish. Then after an hour or so they were off for a martini lunch. Then back for a while until another coffee and Danish break. Finally around four thirty they ran for the train back to the burbs. Almost all the paste up and mechanicals, all the photostats, all the type setting, all the illustration, all the photography, all the stripping of the transparencies and so on were done by different companies and free lancers. Each of these outside sources had their own overhead, management, rent, accounting, and on and on. To make matters even worse, things like photostat houses were unionized. The owners were prohibited from operating their own equipment.

Why didn't someone offer the publishers a less costly alternative by putting all the services under one roof in less costly space? Vence had liked the idea and decided that it should be adapted. He stated that if I was serious he would resign his job. He would join me in implementing my idea. For him this would be a big step. He had one of the top art directing jobs in publishing. Since I was a free lancer it was an easy step for me take, so I agreed.

Westport was the perfect location for our venture. It was on the railroad route between New York and Boston, the sites of most of the big publishers. The Famous Artist Schools was going belly-up. This released a horde of unemployed art talent to supply our needs. We found the ideal home for our new business in an ancient icehouse. It was from the days before refrigeration. The ice had been cut from the pond adjoining it. Then it had been stored, insulated in sawdust, for use during the summer months.

Hollywood could never have surpassed the wonderful, bygone, tranquil atmosphere of our location. To top everything off, the pond was a wonderful place for ice skating in the winter. One of my fondest memories is of ice skating there in a snow storm. It created a magical winter wonderland.

Our business, Publishers' Graphics, grew rapidly. We were able to save publishers a lot of money. We didn't write or edit books or even print them. We did everything in between and we did almost everything in-house. Our new business made a sufficient splash to get us written up in the trade magazines. We soon outgrew the quaint old icehouse.

Publisher's Graphics' new home, was absolutely perfect for our enterprise. It was an old factory. It had been constructed in the early 1800s and stood by the Saugatuck River in Westport. The old brick building consisted of three floors. The two upper floors were lined with paned windows. The building was unique in that the upper floors hung from massive iron bars connected to huge beams at the summit of the structure. This allowed most of the interior space to be unobstructed by supporting walls. I had never seen this type of construction before. I have never seen it since. It worked very well because the old place was standing as sturdy as the day it was built. I could not resist thinking how a simple hacksaw could spell doom to the prodigious structure.

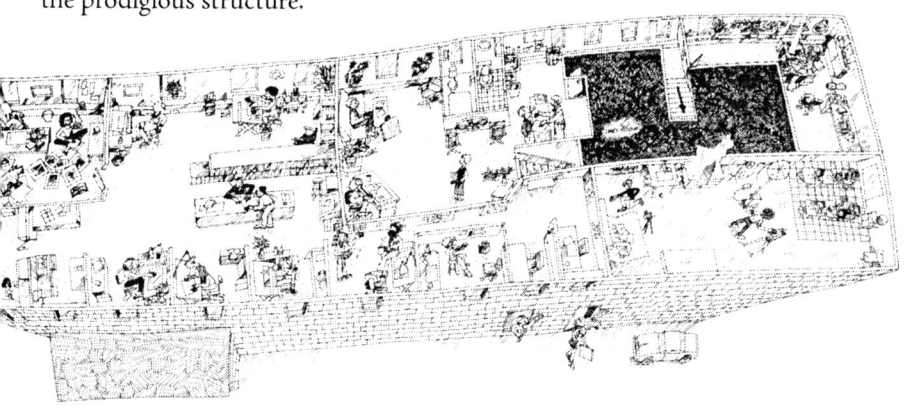

Publisher's Graphics turned an old factory building into a beehive of book production

ancient building had not been occupied for many years. To be perfect for our purposes, alterations were required. First we replaced the old paneled windows with modern windows. An inspection of one of the old window panes confirmed the fact that glass is a liquid. The glass had flowed down and was much thinner at the top than at the bottom.

After other alterations, we were ready to become a book producing factory with a vengeance. We were handling projects that covered thousands of pages of books, usually highly illustrated.

We could call on hundreds of illustrators in addition to the artists we had on staff. We also had a well-equipped photo studio and Photostat room. We even employed an industrial designer to design props and devices that might be needed.

The cherry on our sundae was the location. Our new digs were just a stone's throw from Westport's Saugatuck railroad station. It was on the direct line between New York and Boston. Clients could get off the train almost on our doorstep if they needed to visit us. And as if that was not good enough, there were several excellent restaurants and bars right next door.

We occupied the top two floors of the building. A Ferrari dealer occupied the bottom floor. He was always trying to sell me a Ferrari. I finally convinced him that I couldn't buy a hubcap off of a Ferrari.

One of our clients needed a photograph for a big poster of kids in the hood. They had to be doing something in front of a lot of graffiti on a big wall. The graffiti had to say something specific. In the pre Photoshop days everything could not be easily faked. The photography had to be taken in a controlled environment.

It occurred to me that the big brick walls of our building, which had been painted white, presented a perfect canvas for graffiti. I was on good terms with the manager of the Ferrari dealership. He kindly consented to move his expensive cars in front of the wall for a brief photo shoot. I sent a couple of my guys over to Norwalk to hire a few minority kids. Westport was a bastion of whiteness. This was despite also being a bastion of liberalism, thus the necessity of recruiting in Norwalk.

The graffiti was painted with water paint which was easily removed with a good hosing. So a lot selling some of the world's most expensive cars became for a brief time a center for the under privileged.

Another occasion arose which allowed me some creativity. We were approached by a large publisher who wanted to put out a new elementary math series. They wanted to do something different and asked us what could we come up with. I suggested illustrating the series entirely with photography. My suggestion was greeted with "It would be too expensive."

I responded that it would not be too costly if everything was shot to exact size. If all the transparencies were stripped into place for one shot by the printer. Today, with the aid of computer graphics, doing all this would be "Duck soup." But this was then.

Beginning math books are made up of a lot of "Sets." They are groups of objects. We could hold them together with the use of gravity. This necessitated all the shots being taken from directly above. I had a young industrial designer on staff devise a system. It consisted of overhead tracks and ways to raise and lower cameras precisely. We acquired or already had on hand cameras of every size from 8x10 on down to save film costs. (The size of the print was the size of the camera.)

Every type of generic object of small dimensions known to kids was purchased, from marbles to jelly beans. A problem reared its ugly head over how to define the "Sets." Someone suggested quickly painting swatches on background paper. This was too unwieldy.

It occurred to me that the solution lay in placing some type of white substance such as sugar on a colored background. It could be formed easily with a brush. This idea was poo pooed as unworkable. I was told that we would soon be overrun with ants. Salt too, was vetoed because it would draw moisture and crinkle the background paper.

I dispatched one of our merry band off to shop around for white substances. He produced the solution to our dilemma, Epsom Salts.

When things like marbles and gumdrops would no longer fill the bill, paper sculpture did the job. Everything worked out, we did the first math series ever illustrated completely with photography.

Publisher's Graphics completed the rest of the books in Addison Wesley's science series. I didn't personally do them but they followed the concept of the first book. We did many large projects for dozens of major publishers. I was making good money. The problem for me was that I had to spend too much time on non-creative efforts, things like talking to accountants, things like listening to the gripes of employees about their problems with other employees. Even if I had a creative idea, it was usually carried out by someone else.

The Island

The island was mostly miles of beautiful empty beach

In 1969 it had been over two years since I had last visited my family in South Carolina. I was ashamed that it had been so long between visits. Helen agreed that it was time that we went south. She suggested that we rent a big house on a South Carolina beach and have my family join us. We had spent a vacation years earlier on the beach at Jeykll Island in Georgia. Helen had liked it so much that we almost bought a beach cottage there, but we decided that it was too far from Westport. She was quick to ratify the idea of a house on the shore at Myrtle Beach, South Carolina.

    I called my sister in Greenville, South Carolina and asked her to find a suitable house on the beach in a quiet section of Myrtle Beach. She laughed and commented that I obviously had not been to Myrtle beach in the last few years. The beach had become wall to wall with hotels. She suggested a small island a few miles up the coast called Ocean Isle Beach. It was just over the state line in North Carolina. I told her to put us in touch with a rental agent and she complied. Thus we were introduced to a watershed in the lives of our little family.

Helen was up to her neck in the surf at Ocean Isle when she turned to me and said "This is where I want to be." She had vetoed ideas to buy places in the Virgin Islands, in Spain, in Bequi, at Hilton Head and Jeykll Island. Therefore her announcement carried great weight.

Our first visit to Ocean Isle turned into a joyous family reunion. My parents, plus aunts, uncles, and cousins joined us. Helen had no family other than her parents and her brother. She seemed to love the fact that I had a lot of relatives and she liked them all.

The only house for sale on Ocean Isle was the one we had rented but I procrastinated. When we got back home Helen insisted that I call the realtor and buy it. Alas, it was too late, it had been sold. Helen was determined that we have a house there. If none were for sale then we would have to have one built.

I was too busy to attend to it so Helen went down and bought a lot for us by herself. This was totally out of character for her. She almost never went anywhere without me but she was not to be deterred. Helen purchased a beautiful lot with seventy-five feet of oceanfront. She then came home excited about her purchase.

Our original idea was simply to build a beach cottage, then I discovered that we could build a multiunit building on the lot. A decision was made to build four two-bedroom condo style units. We could rent out the units whenever we couldn't be at the beach.

Ocean Isle was the perfect place for us because it was within easy commuting distance. It was between two airports with jet service to New York. We could also drive down in one long day, yet the climate was little different than that of another day's drive further south because of the proximity to the Gulf Stream.

As soon as I had time, I got to work designing our building. It had to be the best and most modern building on the island. It also had to be accomplished on a limited budget.

I designed a building which was a retro design of an old southern plantation house. I had a model made to show the local builder from Holden Beach, the next beach up from Ocean Isle. Unfortunately, he

Four Winds our first building

delayed for a long time getting started. Then he moved at such a snail's pace that my father had to come to Ocean Isle to take over and have it built.

While he was there I asked him to look out for any other oceanfront property. He called to tell me that he had met a guy who had three oceanfront lots for sale. The guy wanted to buy a car dealership. He wanted $10,000 dollars for each lot. I could only afford to buy two. I offered to buy them if he would throw in a one-year option on the third lot. He agreed and the lots were purchased. A year later the third lot had doubled in value. He honored the option and I bought it.

The first building was renting well so we constructed a twelve-unit building on two of the recently purchased lots. At first I had wanted to name the first building The Poseidon, after the Greek sea god, and use Poseidon's trident as a symbol. Helen objected. She thought Poseidon's trident would be mistaken by some people as Satan's pitchfork.

While sitting in a bar at the airport in Bridgeport, Connecticut I had noticed the name of the bar on a napkin. It said The Four Winds and had a logo of arrows pointing in four directions. The first building had four units so I named it The Four Winds.

The new twelve unit building was named Trade Winds. As new buildings were added they were named Sea Winds, East Winds and West Winds, then we named the whole complex simply The Winds.

It became harder and harder to leave the beach and return home so Helen and I decided to become full time residents of Ocean Isle. This was not an easy decision. It meant leaving our many old friends and our very pleasant Westport lifestyle. But the lure of miles of almost empty beach and the mild climate was not to be resisted. Also our nest was empty, Debbie had gotten married and Gary was off seeking rock stardom. The adventure of a new life beckoned.

Our "Blue State" friends wondered "Who will you talk to down there?" as if "Red State" people were mute. We never had the slightest trouble finding interesting people to engage in conversation.

My half of Publisher's Graphics would have to be sold as well as our house. I told my partner Vence that I would be leaving. I offered to sell him my half of Publisher's Graphics for a very fair price.

His counter offer was insulting. It was accompanied with a threat. If I didn't accept his offer he would take all the employees and clients and set up another company. This was a serious threat. The engine that drove a creative machine like Publisher's Graphics was its talented employees.

I was stunned that someone I had considered a friend would make such an offer and accompany it with a threat.

I hid my anger and stalled in making a response. I used the time to secretly offer for sale my half of the company. The offer was to the two ladies who were second in command, under Vence and myself. They had the loyalty of the rest of the employees. I offered to let them pay me over time. They accepted. It was my partner who was left out in the cold.

Our house was sold along with most of our furnishings. Helen wanted to start out in our new life with new furniture. She wanted furnishings that looked more "Southern." After all our friends' good-bye parties, the time had come to say good-bye to our pleasant years in Westport and embark on our new adventure.

The heirlooms and the treasures that we couldn't part with, along with my books, filled a huge U-haul moving van. I put the gargantuan truck into gear and along with a friend and former employee, Joe Garcias, set off. This was the first time I had ever driven a truck and at times it was a bit terrifying. Heavily laden moving vans don't stop like autos. Sudden light changes can bring on an adrenaline rush.

One act of shear terror I remember was driving down a very narrow road in Brunswick County, North Carolina through the Green Swamp. The road had almost no shoulders with the swamp on both sides. Trucks coming from the opposite direction seemed to clear the van by mere inches.

Somehow we arrived safely and unloaded our vast cargo into a couple of the ground floor units of Four Winds, our first building.

Helen was incredible. She had been born to luxury. She had left a comfortable sprawling house with a guest house and a swimming pool. She had moved into quarters cramped with unpacked boxes. Yet she was happy. I look back on that time fondly. Helen loved to frolic in the ocean. She loved to take long walks on the beach collecting seashells. She loved reading books in shady spots while listening to the sound of the waves crashing on the shore.

There were very few houses on Ocean Isle but they were populated by very interesting people and there were quite a few parties. A lot of the people whose houses were second homes had cocktail parties when they came down to the beach.

Jim and Ann Hesser, a very nice couple lived only a short distance down the beach. Jim was a retired music professor and a very intelligent man. Ann was a very active collector of seashells and had a lot in common with Helen. We had cocktails with them often.

When we didn't have anything else to do after dinner, Helen and I frequently walked a couple of miles down the beach to little store and treated ourselves to Nutty Buddys. We both loved them and it was an excuse for a long beach walk.

I got some kind of muscle ailment, I can't remember what. I was told that there was a medical doctor living at what had been an old boys camp down at the end of the island. I walked down to see him and he fixed me up free of charge. He was a remarkable man. In my discussions with him I found out that he was a professional soldier. He showed me some photos of himself with Che Guevara's body. He told me that he was one of the people who had nailed the notorious Che.

I can't remember his name but it probably wasn't his real name anyway. He was busy doing some body shop work putting a new Volkswagen van into an old body. He was welding some machine guns into the gas tank. The rails on the roof rack would be converted into something special also.

He told me that the purpose of all this was because he was going to set up a house in the Bolivian jungle. He was going to live there while he searched for something. All this had to do with setting up a protective perimeter- changing the van had something to do with getting it through Bolivian customs.

He was a handsome hero right out of the movies. His arm was split open when he ran into a post on the beach one dark night while riding a motorcycle. He sewed up his own injured arm using the hand on his uninjured arm.

Another character I met living on the island was outfitting a small sailboat to sail around the world. He had an Italian name which I can't remember. He was a complete nature nut. He gave us a cake made out of seeds he had collected. We thanked him profusely, but the cake was awful.

Ocean Isle in the early seventies was almost totally unknown to most of the world. The little island had a population of some fifty or so souls. It's hard to imagine my surprise upon meeting a clerk in one of the two small stores on the island who had been in our house back in Westport. He told me he was familiar with every detail of our house. He had spent time in our house because he had dated our baby-sitter. He had lived in New Caanan, a nearby Connecticut town!

I set about designing a house to build on the lot we had exercised the option to buy. The house was designed so that it could be easily converted into six units with a couple of offices on the ground floor. After the house was completed we moved in.

Up till this time all our units, which we called apartments, were rented by a local realtor. Now that we had an onsite office we decided to handle the rentals and operations on our own.

Helen and I knew almost nothing about running a hotel type operation. Helen had a lady who worked for a realtor who handled rentals show her the rudiments. Helen was a quick learner, she set up forms and procedures to run things and to keep track of reservations. She hired one person to help her with office work. She also hired several people for work on Saturdays checking units and making sure they were clean. It was the custom to only rent by the week, and only from Saturday to Saturday. The people renting the units were required to bring their own bed linens or rent them and to leave the units clean upon departure.

After five in the afternoon Helen had no help. She answered the phone taking reservations and preparing dinner at the same time.

Helen Otis Pope was one remarkable lady. She was a direct descendant of John Winthrop, the first governor of the Massachusetts Bay Colony. She was also a direct descendent of James Otis, the patriot who coined the rallying cry of the American Revolution, "No taxation without representation."

Her credentials as a true Yankee were further reinforced by the fact that all her great grandfathers served as officers in the Union Army during the Civil War.

Despite her background, Helen loved the South, especially North Carolina and Brunswick County. She loved her new home with a passion. She was delighted when one of her former classmates at Mount Holyoke College remarked that she had acquired a Southern accent. She was also delighted when she was referred to as, "Miss Helen."

By the early 1970s everyone had heard of the "Outer Banks," but the Southern coast of North Carolina was unknown to the vast majority of people. The road now designated as Highway 179 existed, but it wasn't on any map. It wasn't even on the State map!

Helen accompanied me on a trip to Toronto. The trip had something to do with Addison Wesley, the publishing company. They wanted me to do some work for their Canadian division.

While we were in Toronto we visited the Canadian office of the United States Travel Service. Much to our delight we got in to see the head honcho. While we were there we got him to promise to send us some tour operators from Canada. He later kept his promise and we got a lot of business from one of them.

Helen suggested that we detour on our way back and visit the North Carolina Division of Travel in Raleigh. She wanted to get them to recognize that our area existed.

We went to Raleigh and called on Bill Arnold, the head of the North Carolina Travel Division. He confessed that the state didn't know what to call the coast of Brunswick County.

He further admitted that he couldn't do anything about getting the main road into Sunset Beach and Ocean Isle Beach on the map because that came under the North Carolina Highway Department.

The North Carolina Highway Department only put roads designated as secondary or higher on the map. This was a strict policy, and as politics were involved, they weren't very flexible. It took several years to get Route 179 designated properly and put on the map, but that is another story.

I felt that there was an important need for an organization to promote our area. An opportunity arose to do something about the need. I was invited to attend a meeting of the local Lion's Club. I didn't know but one or two people at the meeting but I got up and stated the need for a chamber of commerce.

Mason Anderson, a local attorney, passed me his card. It requested I call him. This resulted in our having a meeting with a number of prominent business men.

A previous attempt to form a chamber had foundered due to the failure to agree on what to call our area. Helen proposed the name The South Brunswick Islands. The board of the newly-formed Chamber of Commerce adopted it. The State Division of Travel now had a name to promote, and the name is here to stay thanks to an energetic, and forward-thinking lady.

The two of us, with one person to help in the office, were valiantly holding down the fort. I attempted to handle maintenance but I am not one of the world's most handy men. I was a disaster at the job.

Our units had large glass sliding doors and big sliding screens which allowed for an expansive view of the Atlantic. They were made of aluminum so they didn't rust, but the rollers under them were their Achilles heel. They were made of steel and they started to rust almost as soon as they were exposed to the salt air.

One day a guest requested a new screen door as one of theirs had succumbed to the salt. An inspection of our supply revealed one pristine new screen door. I cursed my failure for not procuring more. But I gave thanks for having at least one on hand. I proceeded up to the guests quarters and replaced the kaput screen.

The guests were relieved to have a new door and thanked me for the prompt replacement. A friendly conversation ensued. Upon its

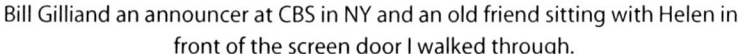

Bill Gilliand an announcer at CBS in NY and an old friend sitting with Helen in front of the screen door I walked through.

conclusion I exited through the last pristine new door. I literally exited through the new egress totally destroying it!

After this, and a few other episodes of incompetence, I was replaced as our maintenance man.

The town of Ocean Isle Beach decided to have a volunteer fire department. The insurance companies required that the department have a minimum number of members to qualify for the lowest rates. The town

My first public speech

population was so small that almost all of us had to become volunteer firemen.

I am overjoyed that some people like serving as volunteer firemen. I am not among them. It is exciting work that engenders adrenaline rushes. However, being summoned in the middle of the night by a phone call to go to a fire was sufficient to cool my ardor.

One fire that I remember was a house aflame inland only a few miles away from Ocean Isle. It was not a big fire and the apparent source of the flames was from a furnace. The fire fighters were standing around pouring great streams of water into the house.

I grabbed a fire extinguisher and went into the house directly to the source of the flames and put it out.

Some people hailed me as a hero. The few who knew better knew that I was simply stupid. I had waded through a lot of water on the floor practically asking to be electrocuted. I later learned that you don't wade through water in a situation like that until the electricity to the building has been turned off.

In addition to serving as a fireman I served on the board of the fire department. It was a boring job but fortunately the board didn't meet often.

At the formal opening of the new fire department I made the first public speech of my life. I can't imagine what kind of high-toned nonsense I laid on the people present. Everyone politely lied and told me what a fine oration I had made.

The public eats up high toned nonsensical verbiage which is probably why I was asked to run for the town council. My ego must have gotten in the way of my common sense because I agreed to run.

My poor gray cells are strained trying to think of things worse than having to spend long boring hours attending things like budget meetings, and having dinner interrupted by telephone calls. Friends on both sides of issues would make requests that would offend either one, one way or the other.

But, once I had committed to friends that I would run, I couldn't get out of it. The opportunity to make some money doing what I wanted to do presented itself. I was offered eighteen thousand dollars to drop out of the race.

I had recently purchased a lot for twenty thousand dollars. Ten percent of the sum had been placed down until the sale closed. I was told that the ten percent would be all that I would owe on the lot.

My reply was that I had heard that everyone has a price but eighteen thousand was not my price. I also said that ten times that was still not my price. If I had a price it would be so high that no one would pay it. I could have made use of the money but I still had a little honor left.

My election was in the bag until the night before the election. "Big Daddy" invited every voter on the island except Helen and me and a few of my diehard friends to a big dinner in one of the island's two restaurants. He was able to persuade enough voters that I was almost a Stalinist, that I would raise their taxes by spending money on foolishness.

The truth was that I am really a libertarian and believe in the least government and the lowest taxes possible. Of course I, like everyone else, hate to loose a contest and have my ego bruised. The bruise however was quickly healed by my relief from having to serve.

Brunswick County had some dirty elections in the early seventies. Votes were bought by giving a "Hauler" two hundred dollars for every twenty votes cast.

The hauler would round up twenty illiterate people in a backward area and bring them to the poles. The "Haulers" kept a hundred dollars for themselves and gave each of the voters who voted "right," five dollars.

The illiterate voter could have someone assist them with voting. If they voted "Correctly," they were given a token. The token, which could be redeemed for five dollars would be a small item like a marble, or an acorn.

I found out how the system worked from a cleaning lady at The Winds. My small contribution to fairness was to pay her a hundred dollars each election not to "haul."

The Winds prospered and new staff and new buildings were added. There was but one cloud that hung over our heads. The fact that all our buildings were on property that was zoned for residential use only. The local "Big Daddy," who controlled the town council and the mayor opposed my getting The Winds property rezoned commercial.

I gained the friendship of several people who were in opposition to dictatorship. Employing similar tactics to those used by the local Fuehrer my buddies temporarily won a majority of the seats on the Ocean Isle Beach town council.

"Big Daddy" controlled things through his daughter, the mayor and his niece, the town clerk. He also used his position as the building inspector.

He had announced that all zoning requests must be submitted to the building inspector. A perusal of the town charter revealed that all zoning requests must be submitted to the zoning committee. A little further research uncovered the fact that the terms of all the members of that august group had expired long ago.

The time for action was at hand. All that was required was to line all the ducks up in a neat row and seize the opportunity!

I knew that success would be followed by a legal assault. Everything done would need to be strictly kosher. A big bad attorney would be required to help me withstand a withering assault of legal bullets.

I consulted a couple of my friends, who I new to be shrewd old-timers, about what lawyer to employ. They both named the same guy because he had kicked their butts on a case they should have won. They said he also was not in "Big Daddy's" pocket.

Henry, the lawyer, gave me the legal requirements. I put the show on the road at the next town council meeting. The carefully orchestrated show began with a friend on the council asking to whom he should give a letter. He told the town council that the letter was addressed to "The chairman of the planning and zoning committee?"

"Big Daddy's statement that the letter should be given to him was greeted with a question. John, my friend, inquired "Are you the chairman of the planning and zoning committee?"

A parliamentary inquiry revealed that all the terms of the members of the planning and zoning committee had long expired. It didn't in fact exist.

The mayor was forced to appoint a new committee. The committee appointed was of course a rubber stamp. She appointed as chairman an old man who could be counted on to do as he was told. But to my advantage he was almost senile.

During this period "Big Daddy" was busy building a golf course. He was almost as rich as God but he was also a skinflint. He had to keep a close eye on every worker lest they not work every second he was paying them. This kept him too busy to worry about me. He was confident that he had put me in my place.

Just before the next council meeting I got word to the stooge chairman that "Big Daddy" wanted the rezoning approved. He also wanted the approval document given to a friend of mine on the council. None of the stooges had attended a council meeting. They knew nothing about the rezoning request so it was approved by them unanimously.

The law required that a notice had to appear in a county newspaper for a couple of weeks. I put the notice in the Southport paper on the other side of the county.

The law also required that a notice be posted in several places. I had an ancient copy machine that produced ancient looking copies. They were crumpled up before they were straightened out for posting.

One of the copies was posted among dozens and dozens of "real" ancient notices at a pier owned by "Big Daddy." Another was placed among a vast number of old notices in a local store. My great coup was placing a notice on the bulletin board in the town hall. There was a clear view of the bulletin board from the town clerk's office. That challenge had to be overcome. The solution consisted of my visiting her on a pretext. Upon leaving the door was closed just enough upon my departure to block her view. The blockage was long enough for me to post the notice among the sea of old notices.

My rezoning request came up at the first town council meeting after the public notice time had expired. The rezoning petition had been added to the agenda at the last moment by one of my friends. "Big Daddy" and his minions were completely taken by surprise! When "Big Daddy" heard that the planning and zoning committee had voted unanimously to approve the rezoning his fury was explosive.

My rezoning was approved by a single vote but that was enough. Law suits were threatened but to no avail. Everything had been done to the letter of the law. The battle was over and things settled back to normal.

Because Ocean Isle Beach and The Winds were virtually unknown, I persuaded an artist's magazine to publicize a trip to The Winds by members of the New York Society of Illustrators.

I supplied the lodging and dining was donated by local restaurants. Complimentary golf was given by courses in the area.

Members of the *Society of Illustrators* arriving

Quite a few members were able to accept our invitation. A top New York photographer and the model of the year accompanied them. A lot of pictures were shot in the area. Everyone had a great time and much publicity was obtained at little cost.

A few months later I thought of yet another publicity stunt. I knew a lot of famous cartoonists who were avid golfers, and the idea occurred to me that a trip bringing a lot of internationally well known figures down to our area would engender major press coverage. It would also go a long way in getting our little chamber of commerce airborne.

I approached Paul Phillips and Bill Arnold the honchos of the North Carolina Travel and Tourism Dept. and they went for it in a big way. Paul suggested giving the trip a long and ridiculous name to get attention. We adapted his name which was something like "The First and Probably the Last Great Brunswick County National Cartoonist Golfing Tour."

Bill Arnold, who was head of the travel division, got the loan of the governor's airplane and once again the local businesses donated their services.

I contacted some of my friends in the National Cartoonist Society and the trip was on. Nothing like this had ever happened in Brunswick County before. The local and North Carolina newspapers covered the trip, some of them like a blanket. The *Charlotte Observer* ran a half page cartoon of *Superman* basking on our beach along with a big story. By every measure the stunt was a big success.

My cartoonist friends left behind a great many cartoons from their visit

Fortune's Smile

Shortly before moving to the island I had received a call. It was from my brother, Tom, who lived in Mission, Texas on the Mexican border. He informed me that stretches of beach on South Padre Island, next to the Mexican border, were being sold off for a bargain price. He told me that I should get down there pronto.

Jim Hillman, a close friend was interested in going to Texas with me and looking things over. We lost no time in departing for Texas. Alas, we were too late!

By the time we arrived the slices of the island were too wide for our meager pocketbooks. The island was being sold by the acre in parcels. They were narrow slices across South Padre. Initially they went across a narrow part of the island and the acreage was small. By the time we got there the strips across the island were wider making the acreage they contained larger. The acreage was too much to afford. Also the parcels for sale were far beyond the existing road.

We stayed on in Mission for a few days. Just before we left for home a new real estate opportunity arose. Tom had found out about an old man who had an eighteen-acre parcel on the main road between Mission and McAllen Texas. It was for sale at a reasonable price. Tom had acquired some inside information: a public golf course was going to be built across the street from the old man's property.

We made an offer and it was accepted. As soon as I got back to Westport I went to work designing a housing development for our new acquisition.

I had an industrial designer, who was employed by Publisher's Graphics, build me a model of my development design. He did a terrific job and was able to accede to my request that it fold up to a size that would fit under the seat on a plane.

Armed with the model and plans, Jim and I again flew to Texas. We presented the model and our ideas for the development to the local planning board. It received enthusiastic approval.

All the ducks were in a row but I got cold feet. In order to finance the construction Jim and I would have to pledge all our assets. After a mostly sleepless night I had to tell Jim that I just couldn't risk my property in North Carolina.

I told him that he could have all the work I had done and my half of the property for only what I had paid. Jim said he understood my position and that it was fine with him. He stated that he would just as soon we put our land up for sale. He felt that we probably would make a profit.

We once again returned back to Westport and forgot about our venture. The venture arose again when Jim visited Helen and I soon after we had moved to Ocean Isle.

Jim had gotten married and was living in California. A business trip brought him to Carolina. He made an excursion down to the island to visit Helen and me. This visit was the only one he was able to make for many years. By a strange coincidence he was standing next to me enjoying a cocktail when the phone rang. We had just been conversing about our Texas adventure.

The voice on the phone was my brother Tom in far away Mission, Texas. He related the good news that he had an offer in hand for our land down there. It was more than twice what we had paid for it. The affirmative reply was almost instantaneous.

Jim stated that he liked the look of things in the area. He suggested that rather than send him his half I take our money and buy us a tract of local land. The idea was eagerly ratified by me. Soon after his departure I embarked on a land search.

I approached, John Williams, a friend and a real-estate broker. I told him that I had just sold a tract of land in Texas with a friend. We had decided to roll the money by investing in some local land.

John showed me a number of tracts but nothing looked like a steal. Little did I know that anything bought in this area back then would be a steal!

I called Jim and told him that nothing I found "floated my boat" and I sent his money to him.

I was busy with other things and I forgot about looking for land. Months later I received a call from John Williams whose opening words were, "Are you interested in the real-estate buy of a lifetime?"

This query carried the impact of a salvo from a battleship. I knew John to be a very serious, conservative type who carefully measured his words.

His phone call lead to a meeting with John and three others, John's father in law, Harris Thompson, Paul Dennis and Ed Gore. Even though I had not met the other guys I was invited to join them in the purchase of a big hunk of land at a bargain price. It was a seven-hundred

A pen and ink drawing of the Sea Trail waterfront

acre tract from the International Paper Company. The tract ran for several miles around Sunset Beach. It included a vast amount of frontage on the U.S. Intracoastal Waterway.

The need for more collateral compelled them to seek one more partner. I suppose that my having told John that I desired to roll some Texas money had led him to believe that I was loaded. In reality that was not the case. But it led to my good fortune in being a twenty-five percent owner in a prize tract of land.

I was sworn to secrecy and given less than twenty-four hours to decide and produce my share of the earnest money. My new partners were afraid that 'Big Daddy" would find out about the sale and grab it for himself.

There was no time to look over the land. In any case it would have been next to impossible. It was covered by intense growth that was very much like a jungle. I didn't need to look it over. It was so well located and of such vast acreage that it was indeed a great bargain. Helen readily concurred with my decision to go for it.

Paul Dennis was a genius when it came to land development. He went right to work. He was a natural born leader, and since he was freely willing to devote his time and expertise to the project he was elected President of the new corporation.

I suggested the name "Sea Trail" because the old King's Highway went right through our new property. The locals called the narrow path, "The Old Stage Trail." This was one of the only places where the ancient highway ran along next to the sea.

I knew from my experiences in advertising, that it was more distinctive to use two words that don't normally go together than something like "Buena Vista" or "Oakwood." My new partners liked the name so Sea Trail was adapted.

Paul, Harris Thompson and John Williams were in the mobile

home business. They wanted to start off with a development of mobile home lots. Ed and I went along. Our first development, Seaside Station consisted of mobile home lots.

Seaside Station got off to a successful start. Only a few months later we purchased several hundred more acres from the International Paper Company.

Soon after this we were approached by Larry Young, a very successful builder of golf courses. Larry wanted to lease enough land to build a golf course. He had only recently completed Marsh Harbour Golf Course. It was one of the most beautiful in the country. We knew he would build something special, and he did!

Soon after Oyster Bay, the new course, opened it was proclaimed by *Golf Digest* to be "The best new resort course in the United States."

Larry had selected a rising star among golf course architects, Dan Maples, to design a new course. He wanted to build it at Sea Trail.

We told Larry that we had decided to build the

Oyster Bay the first golf course

course ourselves and that we would like to use Dan to design it. Larry said that it was okay with him, so we hired Dan and went to work.

The golf courses caused a major change in direction for the corporation. We went upscale. All our property except Seaside Station became Sea Trail Plantation.

The Old Post Road ran right through the area where Dan was designing the new course. I felt that at least some of it should be left in its old location. Dan cleverly preserved quite a bit of it by having a cart path follow it. The old road was only as wide as a cart path.

Most of the property was covered by growth so dense that it reminded me of the Peten Rain Forrest in Guatemala. However, Paul Dennis, who was supervising the construction, always knew exactly where he was. I would have thought he was secretly using a global positioning

Most of the property was a jungle

The cart path along much of the tenth fairway on the *Maples* golf course follows the path of the old road that went all the way to to Boston in New England. George Washington came down it in 1791

device but they did not exist at that time.

I remember being terrified hearing the sound of a giant bulldozer only a few feet away and not being able to see it.

Paul had selected a site for the clubhouse but no clubhouse had been designed. In fact no one knew what size or type of clubhouse we needed. We visited a number of resorts looking at clubhouses. Time was running out and we were still going around in circles.

Time was running out in two ways. First, the course could be finished with no clubhouse. Two, the tax depreciation law was about to change for commercial property. After a rapidly approaching, date it would take more than thirty years to depreciate the clubhouse instead of eighteen.

I had discovered years before that the only way to get a group to make a decision on a design was to put a point of departure in front of them on paper. Then if they like it or don't like it you can get them to say what they like or don't like. Then you can narrow things down until hopefully a decision can be made.

We couldn't go to an architect until we could tell him what we wanted. I asked my brother, a builder, to give me one weekend of his time to help me come up with a point of departure. He agreed but stipulated that after one weekend he was going to charge for his time.

We put aside everything else and went to work. Fortunately, by the end of a weekend with little sleep we had designed a large building. I asked each of the partners to drop by and look the plans over. They complied with my request.

John Williams and Harris Thompson said that they liked it. Ed Gore said he liked it if we could turn the main stairway to the side, which was no trouble. Paul Dennis asked Tom how much he would want to build it. Tom said cost plus ten percent. Paul Dennis said "Build it" and left.

Back then a commercial building could be built without an architect. Tom and I had thought that we were only designing a building so that we could give an architect an idea of what was wanted.

Tom immediately went to work. The work went on for sixty hours a week for many weeks and then the clubhouse was completed. It was finished one day before the tax law changed. The Maples Clubhouse, as the golf course had been named after its architect, was opened to much fanfare. There was a big party with a steel drum band and a lot of refreshments. The local newspaper put out a special supplement about it.

The clubhouse was one of the grandest buildings in the county when it was built. It has since been surpassed by a great many larger and grander structures. But it still stands in it's quiet splendor and continues to deliver service to golfers.

Life had been good for Helen and I. We had traveled to Europe many times and had taken a number of month-long trips with John and

The Maples clubhouse

Francis Williams. We had spent a month in the islands of the Caribbean, a month traveling around Mexico, a month traveling around the islands of Hawaii and a month in England.

In addition to these long jaunts we spent a large amount of time at board meetings of a few days duration at the top resorts throughout the southeast. We attended board meetings and were entertained on cruise ships and even on a Mississippi steamer. For a long time I served on eleven tourism related boards of directors. There were so many meetings at top resorts that the dates often conflicted. Almost always we were charged little or nothing and wined and dined and entertained lavishly.

I loved Helen passionately and we were so happy together and life was so good that I feared that everything was too wonderful. I worried about the old warning that " Into each life a little rain must fall." The rain

We attended Board and club meetings in many parts of the world. Shown here are only a few. Acapulco, Nova Scotia, Puerto Rico, Switzerland, and a private Caribbean Island.

Helen on her last trip to Bequi

fell! Helen was stricken with Alzheimer's.

At first I tried to have us carry on as before. I now believe that was a mistake. It subjected her to situations that were stressful to her. Fortunately though, before her cruel disease got too bad, I took Helen and all ten members of our family on a long trip. We all went to Bequi, her favorite Caribbean island. It was a last hurrah. She seemed to enjoy being there with her children and her grandchildren.

Under no circumstances was I going to permit Helen to go to a nursing home. I didn't care what it took, she was going to stay in her own house. I wouldn't listen when people told me that I must put her in a nursing home. Everything that could hurt her was put away, When I wasn't watching her, a nurse was.

My mind was abruptly changed when I noticed her nurse was fussing with something in her bedroom. Then I saw Helen in the kitchen with a sharp knife in her mouth. She had it in a glass and was sucking on it thinking it was a soda straw! I don't know how she found the knife but I knew then that she was not safe at home.

With the help of our daughter, Debra, I mounted a search for a nursing home. We visited and researched facilities far and wide before settling on a nursing home in Conway, South Carolina. It was too far away for daily visits but light-years above all the other choices. I vowed to spend every Sunday with her and I kept my vow for all of the twelve years she had left.

Helen never complained and was always cheerful. She reminded me of a great big lovable doll.

So there was no choice, I had to put her in a nursing home. They took better care of her than she could have ever gotten at home and she was safe. But it didn't matter, I always felt like a rat for putting her in a nursing home.

While it rained on our personal life, fortune smiled on our business ventures. The Winds had increased in size to include sixteen

The oceanfront pool at *The Winds*

The *Jones/Byrd* clubhouse with the *Carolina Conference Center* in the distance at Sea Trail Plantation

buildings, a lot of ocean frontage and a staff of nearly fifty people.

Over the next few years Sea Trail Plantation continued to grow. More land was purchased until the total reached over two thousand acres. Two more golf courses were built and named after their architects. Four more clubhouses of various types were built. Hundreds of houses and condominiums were constructed. Today, Sea Trail is one of the top golf resorts in the Southeast.

I would have swapped it all in an instant to have Helen back as she was.

It was lonely living in a great big house without her, but I was lucky. I had a loving family and a lot of good friends nearby. I also had a lot of work to keep me busy.

One night, approaching dawn, I was awakened by a banging on my bedroom door. Upon opening the door, a sheriff's deputy and my next door neighbor greeted me. My burglar alarm had been going off wakening the neighborhood for the last thirty minutes. I don't hear very well and I am a deep sleeper. In fact, I could probably sleep through a rock concert. I had given my neighbor a key to my house and the security code lest the alarm go off in my absence.

After that incident my imagination instilled a fear. A fear that someone could enter my house and bring about my demise with impunity. I possessed a thirty eight caliber revolver, which had been purchased years before. It was loaded with hollow point bullets. I felt that if I had to shoot some son of a bitch I wanted to be sure I blew a big hole in him. Little did I know that the recipient of one my hollow point bullets would be me!

I had placed the revolver in my large bed on the far side. There was no round in the chamber. The pistol would have to be cocked or the cylinder would have to have revolved before it would fire. It was handy and I thought it was safe.

In the middle of the night a few months later I was abruptly awakened. I had a hole as big as a silver dollar in my leg very near my groin. It was spouting a lot of blood which I attempted to staunch with a pair of underpants. I didn't realize it at the time that my leg had a matching hole on the exit side. I was in shock but I managed to call 911 before lying back on the bed. Then I remembered that the front door was locked and the alarm was on.

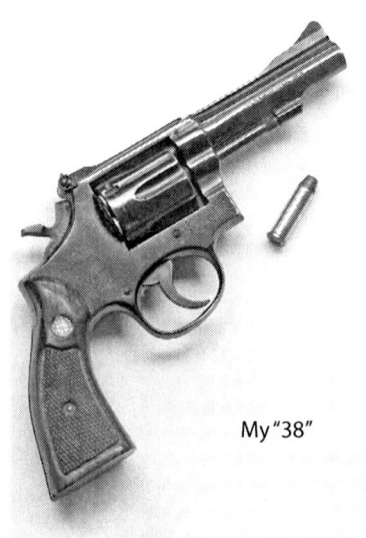

My "38"

Once again I arose and spouting blood, I staggered down the hall and unlocked the door and turned the alarm off. The ambulance arrived and I was whisked to the hospital.

The next thing I remembered was my brother, Tom, talking to me in the hospital. My main concern was people finding out about my stupidity in having a loaded pistol in bed with me. I told Tom to put it out on the street that I was shot by a jealous husband. He informed me that that story wouldn't fly. One of the guys in the ambulance was a friend. All I could do was make light of my stupidity. I remembered the old adage about laughing about yourself and the world laughs with you. Otherwise they laugh at you!

Gunshot wounds are not stitched up for some reason. They require a lot of bandaging. After being discharged from the hospital I required the frequent visits of a nurse to change the bandages. I was fortunate in having the medical services of a pretty young lady who possessed a good sense of humor.

I have always been a bit modest but the wound's close proximity to my groin forbade modesty in treating my injury. The pretty young nurse upon observing my injury stated "You are lucky, you almost shot your wing wang off!"

I am proud of my immediate retort ,"It is well that it made such a small target!"

After the holes closed up I had to have some surgery to remove the scorched skin cause by the powder burns that resulted from the muzzle almost abutting my leg. Soon I was as good as new and my gross stupidity was history.

During the weeks spent in healing, my daughter, Debra, and my son, Gary, took over visiting their mother. It is a shame how many people are just stashed in nursing homes and forgotten.

My grief was so stressful that I acquired an ulcer. Time and medicines brought my stress under control but it was renewed when Helen

Helen in happy times

died in November of 2003.

I have lost the great romantic love of my life. But she has left me with more than my share of fond memories. Also she has left me the greatest treasure one can possess, beautiful, wonderful and loving children and grandchildren.

In my final years a love of another kind has been reawakened, my love of drawing and illustration. It is the love that I had as a small boy back in Johnson City and Boone's Creek more than seventy years ago.

After many years of being concerned with making money I made a big discovery. I discovered that when one's needs are assured, it is ridiculous to chase the buck. It is especially foolish when one's needs are simple. After all, you can only eat one meal at a time and you can only sleep in one bed each night.

When you live in a beautiful place by the sea anywhere you might go is not as beautiful as where you are, when you have seen just about every place you wanted to see, when you are too old for adventure, why endure the travails of travel?

With all this in mind, I gave most of my property to my children and let them take over running things. I decided to get back to my first love, art. I tried painting pretty pictures but painting a pretty picture does not offer the same challenge for me as creating an illustration.

My problem was that there was nothing to illustrate. That was solved by a chance conversation that I had with an attractive young lady in a local bookstore. One of my many failings is my propensity to stick my nose in other peoples business. I have an almost insatiable curiosity and it led me to inquire about the book business.

I inquired of the young lady. "What kind of book do you wish you had to sell?"

Her almost instantaneous response was "A history of Brunswick County."

Almost without thinking, I said "I'll write one." The thought of writing a book had never entered my head. I had no academic credentials but I was a complete history nut. I had even been a member of The Company of Military Historians for a number of years. Plus I had a friend, Jack DeGroot, who I knew would help me out. Jack had written eight successful novels. She is not only a very attractive young lady, she is an excellent writer.

The best part about doing the book is that I would get to illustrate it. Almost immediately I set to work and I enjoyed the task so much that I had to force myself to stop and go to bed lest I sleep until noon the next day. Having read many hundreds of non-fiction, history books, combined with my memory, the internet and interviews with old timers, supplied most of the needed research. Visits to historic sites and the local library were also a great help.

It did not matter to me that a local history would have only local appeal because money was not my motive. I felt that I was doing a service for a place that I love and that has been very kind to me.

From the introduction of LisaPaint on Lisa, the predecessor of the MacIntosh computer, I had experimented with computer graphics. As the years passed, computer graphics became more sophisticated. I was able to do more and more complicated work on the computer. For a number of years all I could do was produce brochures, ads and simple drawings for The Winds.

Recently the introduction of very powerful computers, sophisticated software and computer pressure sensitize tablets with electronic wands has made it possible to paint on the computer. Painting with an electronic wand on a computer tablet even feels like using a real brush. Speed in mixing colors is one of the major advantages of electronic painting.

Of course the painter must be able to paint and draw conventionally as well as having additional computer knowledge, but there is no cleanup time required. Also mistakes can be easily undone and colors can be completely changed just as easily.

I was able to incorporate several old illustrations that I had done in the past in the book *Tales of the Silver Coast, A Secret History of Brunswick County*. The other illustrations were painted and drawn on the computer.

My novelist friend, Jack DeGroot, edited the book and wrote five chapters in the book for me. The publisher, Barbara Brannon with the assistance of Nickie Leone organized the book and made sure details such as properly attributing sources and quotes were checked and rechecked.

Due largely to the efforts of the aforementioned talented people the first book was a success. It was so much fun that I decided to do another.

This time I decided to do a full-color book about pirates. I couldn't think of anything that would be more fun to illustrate than pirates. I had gained enough confidence from the first book to write it by myself although Barbara Brannon was a major help.

It was also enjoyable to research and write about pirates. This great labor of love required almost 150 illustrations. It was a lot of work but I enjoyed every minute spent on it.

Once again I was able to incorporate several old illustrations that I had done in the past, but mostly the illustrations were painted on

My books so far

my computer. One illustration deserves special comment.

The movies are going all out producing historical epics with casts of thousands that are actually digital people. It is so easy to create "Real" people and objects on computers that movie directors find it difficult not to go overboard.

Movie special effects companies with the help of computers with massive power can create very lifelike crowds of people and objects. For example, first they create one figure. Then they create ten actions and then apply the ten different actions to ten copies of the figure. Next they create another figure and apply the same ten actions to ten copies of the figure. After they have created ten different original figures they have a crowd of one hundred. The movie viewer is totally fooled. If the director wants an army of one thousand, all he needs is ten copies of the one hundred and so on.

On the Mac computer all one needs to do to copy a selection is to "Option" click it with the mouse. I went to see the movie *Troy* with a fellow Mac user and even though I hate talking in a movie I couldn't resist a comment. Helen of Troy may have had a face that launched a thousand ships but it seemed like her face launched more like ten thousand in this flick. I turned to my buddy and whispered "Option click, option click". He laughed.

For one illustration in the pirate book I needed to depict almost two thousand buccaneers on their way overland to plunder a Spanish city. In the old days this would have been a formidable task.

I decided to employ my Mac to ease the job. After all if the movie people can use the computer to produce mobs of people why can't I?

Several little running pirates were jotted down in pencil on a scrap of paper and scanned into the computer. Next I painted them in black and white based on my sketches. There was no need to use color at this point as I was going to vary the colors on each figure to add more variety.

The next step involved copying and pasting my murderous villains in random order into my background. Some of my copies were behind the others and were slightly reduced in size to give the illusion of depth. The bestowal of varied colors of clothing, headgear and footwear as well as varied weaponry in the hands of the cruel cutthroats completed my cast of thousands. All that was needed to place the bloodthirsty mob in Central America was the addition of a couple of palm trees.

One of my treasured possessions has for most of my life been a copy *Howard Pyles Book of Pirates*. His illustrations are truly works of art and my feeble efforts are pitiful by comparison. Pyle's illustrations have been used along with the same bunch of ancient steel engravings to

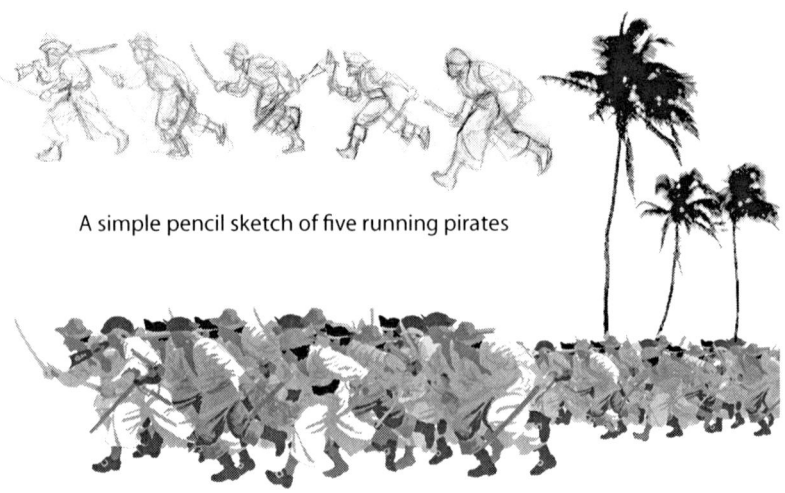

A simple pencil sketch of five running pirates

Becomes hundreds of running pirates

illustrate just about every pirate book for nearly a century. I don't pretend to be in a class with Howard Pyle. However I decided that it was time, in this day of superior color reproduction to do another pirate book with all new illustrations. I have titled it *Miller Pope's Book of Pirates* as a salute to the master of pirate illustration, Howard Pyle.

Before finishing the pirate book I had already been putting together ideas for this book. And as I work on this one I have another in mind. The rest of my life shall be spent writing and illustrating books whether anyone reads them or not.

The beautiful blue natural spaceship upon which we are all passengers has made more than eighty circumnavigations of our life giving star since I came aboard. My trip has been very enjoyable for the most part despite some bumps. I can't help but ponder how lucky I have been to have had such great traveling companions, a loving wife and the two wonderful children she gave me, and the four loving grandchildren they gave me. Also, among the passengers, there were the many good and kind people who enriched my life with their aid, their cheerfulness, and their friendship.

There were many forks in the road. What would have happened if I had taken even one fork different? As the Dylan song goes, "The answer my friend lies blowing in the wind."

Lightning Source Inc.
LaVergne, TN USA
14 August 2009
154871LV00003B/9/P